YESTERDAY'S JOURNEY

I0456754

David Berardelli

YESTERDAY'S JOURNEY

GRAVESTONE PRESS

A GRAVESTONE PRESS PAPERBACK

© Copyright 2017
David Berardelli

The right of David Berardelli to be identified as author
and channel of this work has been asserted by him in
accordance with the Copyright, Designs and Patents Act
1988.

All Rights Reserved

No reproduction, copy or transmission of the publication
may be made without written permission.

No paragraph of this publication may be reproduced,
copied or transmitted save with the written permission of
the publisher, or in accordance with the provisions of the
Copyright Act 1956 (as amended).

Any person who does any unauthorised act in relation to
this publication may be liable to criminal prosecution
and civil claims for damages.

ISBN: 978 1 78695 758 0

Gravestone Press
is an imprint of
Fiction4All
www.fiction4all.com

This Edition
Published 2022

Chapter 1

His picture pressed snugly against her bosom, she sat alone in the heavy darkness of her bedroom, letting the fresh tears warm her cheeks.

She'd made the room dark because she didn't want to see anything. Her bed, the apartment window, her closet—everything about her room, her surroundings, reminded her of him. Darkness was the only way she knew to keep it away. To prevent it from devouring her.

She also experienced a sense of peace in the darkness. And a warm silence, which she desperately needed right now. She was content just to sit there all alone, her eyes closed, letting the silence and the peace caress and warm her.

She could no longer force herself to look at his picture. Having it pressed against her bosom gave her a sense of warmth, of security, but she could no longer bear to look at his face. She couldn't stand to be reminded of how handsome he was, how full of life… How wonderful he'd made her feel when she gazed into his beautiful dark-brown eyes. She could no longer bear to see his smile. The crinkly laugh-lines that gathered around his eyes whenever something caught his fancy. The tiny crescent-shaped dimple on the right side of his mouth that showed so faintly whenever his mouth edged gradually in that direction for one of his sexy half-smiles.

It had been six weeks since the nightmare. A day she would never forget. It was a day like any other, starting with breakfast and her usual twenty-minute drive to the bank on Penn Avenue in downtown Pittsburgh. But just a few hours later, the day—as well as her world—had turned dark and cold and terrifying the instant a few soft, well-chosen words had wrenched her heart out of her chest to turn her life into the shambles it had become since that horrible day.

She'd cried every hour of every day ever since. This day should be no different, should it? But somehow, it was. Somehow, it felt different. The tears continued to drift down her cheeks, but right now she had the strange feeling that one day the well would eventually run dry altogether.

Somehow, that did not seem very likely. The grief was there. It had set up shop and intended to remain for an extended stay.

Why shouldn't the tears continue as well?

The first few moments right after she had been given the horrifying news had been a blur. Her mind was trying to cope with the shock by bathing everything in a soft shade of gray. By doing this, it somehow softened the blow, made it less painful. Less devastating. Otherwise, she might have collapsed. Or suffered a heart attack.

She'd been working at her cage that morning. She just finished a transaction and closed her drawer. She remembered finishing up with Mrs. Dillinger, the nice, quiet old lady who came in once a month to deposit her pension check. Just moments after she'd sent the gentle lady on her way, Mr. Engel, the bank president, walked over very quickly. In his usual soft, high-pitched whisper, he asked her to accompany him to his office. He'd looked so pale, so grim and morose. He always wore dark suits, spent considerable money on his nails and thinning gray hair and looked very much like a mortician. However, on this particular day, he seemed even gloomier than usual.

Her first reaction, of course, was that she had done something wrong. As she followed her boss's tall, slender frame down the carpeted hall, her mind instantly looped, going back to all the things she'd done during the last few days. A miscalculation, perhaps? Or maybe she hadn't accurately recorded the correct amount for her tallies the day before.

She found herself worrying about that extra break she'd taken the afternoon before. Derek had asked her to pick up something for him at the drugstore across the street. What was it? Benydril? Ibuprophen? She remembered that it was definitely Benydril. His sinuses had been acting up lately. And it had to be the non-drowsy kind so he could take it during working hours.

The errand had only taken her ten minutes. And since she'd done it during a slow time, when most of their customers had gone back to work after lunch, she didn't think there would be a problem. All the cashiers did quick errands during the day. Mr. Engel was strict, but he'd never been one to quibble about such minor issues.

Even so, she was nervous about what she might have done. Why Mr. Engle looked so glum. When she worried about something, her mind tended to go blank, turning everything hazy and indistinct. This time, the blankness had, for some reason, eclipsed that important detail. That tiny sliver that would shed light on the situation, telling her what she'd done. Even so, she couldn't help feeling nervous and somewhat frightened as she followed her boss into his office, where the words *Ronald L. Engel, Bank President*, showed in bold black letters on a shiny square silver plaque over the polished cedar door.

In no time at all, she would realize that this emergency meeting had nothing whatsoever to do with bank business. Or that tiny errand the day before.

Derek was dead.

Her fiancé, the love of her life, had been shot and killed in a botched burglary at a 7-Eleven just two blocks away.

Derek Manning, the handsome loving man who, in just eight weeks, would have become her husband, had been shot and left for dead by an armed robber less than half a mile away.

According to what Mr. Engel had been told by the police, the senseless crime had taken place just half an hour earlier. Just a few minutes before that, she'd just taken her break, gone to the ladies' room and slipped into the break room for a cup of vanilla coffee so she could sit down and enjoy her glazed doughnut.

All the while, her beloved soulmate lay bleeding to death on the filthy floor of the 7-Eleven a mere two blocks down the street...

A fresh batch of tears came back, covering her cheeks with warmth.

Even after six weeks, she still couldn't accept it, couldn't come to terms with the fact that Derek was dead. Even after the showing, the funeral services and the burial, she still couldn't admit to herself that

Derek was no longer here with her. That he'd never come to see her again. That she'd never again feel his arms around her, his warm lips on hers. Never again would he tell her in his soft, special whisper how much he loved her, how much she meant to him, what they would do once they were married. Where they'd live. How many kids they should raise…

Derek was gone, but she didn't want to believe it. Or think it. Or say it. Or even whisper it…

Not even to herself.

Whispering it, saying it aloud would make it real, and she didn't want it to ever be real. It had somehow become less real in the darkness, less horrifying in the silence.

But she couldn't ignore that one cold, undeniable fact. He hadn't come for her in the last six weeks. Hadn't talked to her. Or called her. Or shown himself. It told her the horrible truth. That even though she could never accept what had happened, she would one day have to stand in front of the mirror, look at herself and say it.

But not now.

Maybe not even tomorrow. Or the day after. Or next week.

Right now, darkness suited her best. It kept everything away—the grief, the sadness, the agony. She knew she couldn't escape what happened, but the darkness somehow insulated her from all of it, keeping it far enough away. At least for right now.

She sat curled up in her chair and let the numbing sensation take over once again. Hopefully, she would fall asleep. If not, she'd take another pill. The last six weeks, she had taken a pill each night. Otherwise, she'd be forced to spend another night fully awake in this very chair, the one Derek had bought her just three months ago for her thirty-second birthday. Another long, excruciatingly lonely night of sitting here, thinking about him, and reliving their two-year relationship.

Keeping her wet eyes tightly shut, she used one hand to clutch the velvety arm of the chair. It was the same arm Derek had gripped dozens of times earlier while he knelt facing her, smiling lovingly at her, telling her how much he loved her.

I love you, Paula. I always have, always will.

Even now, after all that had happened, she could still hear his loving words caressing her. It was like a warm breeze flowing gently in the moonlight.

Just then, someone knocked quietly on her door.

As always, she ignored it. It was probably Mom or Dad. She didn't want to see them right now. She didn't want to see anyone right now.

Except Derek. And she knew it wasn't him.

Or *was* it?

Was there even one slim chance in a million that he'd actually come back to see her?

Anything was possible. Derek had said that before—many times. He'd said that when you truly loved someone, nothing was impossible. There would always be a connection. A constant blending of two souls that would survive as long as their love remained strong. He also said that something as wonderful as true love could never really die.

Perhaps he was right. Perhaps even after the agonizing horror of what had happened, something good could come out of this. Something wonderful. Something miraculous.

Something that would never die.

But even as the dark, cold terror slithered toward her, reminding her that what had happened six weeks ago was very, very bad, that she would never see Derek again, something else struggled to show itself. This sensation was bright and warm, and felt wonderful. It kept telling her that the last six weeks hadn't happened at all. That there was a chance after all that Derek would indeed call on her again.

It was this bright, warm sensation that made her open her eyes and turn toward the door. For nearly half a minute, she struggled to see into the darkness, hoping to visualize a glimmer of Derek's face, his eyes. For one instant, she thought she might have seen something. Then realized it was just her imagination.

There was nothing.

Another quiet knock.

Sighing, she cleared her throat. "Y-Yes?"

The door opened. A slim vertical beam of harsh yellow light widened slowly.

"Paula baby?" A dark ball penetrated the beam of light almost in mid-center. Mom poked her head in the doorway.

Her heart sank. "Yes, Mom?"

"Baby, we were wondering if…if you'd like some dinner…"

"No, thanks."

Her mother sighed. "Baby, you haven't eaten in—"

"I'm really not hungry, Mom."

11

"Listen, Paulie, I can understand what you're going through. We all can. We can because we've been going through this with you. But you've really got to eat something. It's been several days. You haven't eaten enough to keep a bird alive. It's been two days since you sat with us at the kitchen table. You only picked at your food, and—"

"I'm all right, Mom…"

"No, dear. You're *not* all right. You've got to keep up your strength…"

"Mom, I really don't wanna talk about this or anything else right now."

"Paula baby…"

"Mom, please respect my wishes and just leave me be." It was so difficult, keeping the heat of anger, frustration, and heartbreak inside. She wanted so much to let it all out. To scream. To shriek. And force the badness and the anger and the panic out of her spirit in one gigantic burst. Her heart thundered as she watched her mother's dark silhouette remain in the doorway those few tense seconds before it finally withdrew and was replaced by the beam of light. Then, finally, the beam grew slender once again. A moment later, it disappeared entirely and turned right back into the comforting darkness that made her sigh in instant relief.

The door clicked quietly shut. The silence came right back to soothe and protect her.

The terror all snug and comfortable inside her once again, Paula closed her eyes and sat back. Derek's photo still pressed snugly against her bosom, she let the darkness overpower her and take her gently into a soft shade of hazy grayness.

12

Chapter 2

Derek, his boyishly handsome face bright and happy, came to her in her dream.

As if watching a movie, she saw the two of them sitting together in the tall grass, their arms entwined as they kissed passionately beneath the stars. Derek's beautiful dark-brown eyes twinkled in the moonlight as he held her in his arms. His mouth very close, he told her he'd never leave her, that they'd always be together. Their love was pure and true. Not even death could separate them.

They kissed again. Afterward, Derek whispered something else. However, his voice had become so soft that she couldn't understand what he'd said. She tried moving closer. He suddenly vanished, becoming one with the darkness of the night. For long moments she sat there all alone, looking around frantically while trying to see an image of him in the darkness. There was nothing. No sign of his face, his eyes, his smile. Just the memory of that last delicious lingering kiss.

Frustrated, she gazed up at the starry sky and wondered where he'd gone. The stars told her nothing as they glittered happily amidst the infinite blackness of the sky.

Moments later, she opened her eyes. Her stiff neck and throbbing joints told her that she'd slept in the chair once again. She'd slumbered alone among its soft cushions, his photo still face-down against her bosom.

Remembering her dream, she quickly scanned the room.

Once again, she realized she was alone. As much as she wanted to see his image, Derek was nowhere among the darkness.

Frustrated, she pushed herself up. Ignoring her stiffness and the sudden pain of her circulation returning, she looked around the small room a second time. The bed was made and hadn't changed its appearance since the day before. She'd been here most of yesterday, staring up at the ceiling for several hours before dozing off. But nothing had changed. It was just as she had feared. Derek hadn't come back.

However, the darkness that had clung so tightly to her the night before had dimmed. It was no longer quite as heavy or consuming.

A new day, perhaps?

It really didn't matter. For the last six weeks, all the days had meshed into a single gooey lump of painfully dark, dismal agony. It didn't matter how many of them there were or how many would follow. The only thing that truly mattered to her was that she faced the rest of her life alone. A life without Derek standing beside her, holding her, comforting her, and loving her. In a matter of just a couple of frantic heartbeats, her existence had turned into a bone-chilling bleakness that made her shudder each time she drew a breath.

A knock at the door. Mom again?

She sighed. She knew better than not say anything. Mom was stubborn. She was also very worried. She'd stay close to the door until she was confident Paula was all right. If she suspected something had gone wrong, she wouldn't hesitate to come in.

"Yes?"

The door creaked open a few inches. "Honey?"

"Yes, Mom?"

"Would you like breakfast this morning? Maybe some toast and coffee?"

Her first reaction was to tell her mother she wasn't interested. However, the moment she thought of that, she heard Derek's soft voice in her head. *"You can't stay here all by yourself forever, baby doll…"*

She scanned the room once again. Was Derek actually speaking to her? Had his spirit somehow managed to remain close to her even after death? Had he decided to stick around to make sure she was safe? That nothing bad happened to her in his absence? Was he worried that she'd have difficulty adapting to her frightening new situation? Did he want to hold off on his passing over until he was confident she was ready to face the rest of her life without him at her side?

Or was it just something else she'd imagined?

Derek wouldn't want her living like this, grieving like this. He wouldn't want her to shut herself off from the world. From life, from all the good things they'd both known and loved. He'd want her to start living again. He wouldn't want her to sit in this room forever, dying inside a little as each second passed, his picture pressed tightly against her bosom, her eyes closed as the tears stained her cheeks.

15

"Paula dear?"

Mom's voice startled her, bringing her back once again from her self-imposed darkness.

"Yes, Mom?"

"Breakfast? Maybe just some toast? Coffee? I just made a fresh pot of French vanilla, just the way you like it…"

"Maybe…maybe I would like some coffee, Mom," she said even before she realized it.

"That's fine, dear." Mom sounded pleased. "Just c'mon out when you're ready."

"Okay…" She waited until the door closed. Then, reluctantly, she slowly disengaged herself from the chair. It was difficult. She'd been sitting in the same position since yesterday afternoon. Before that, she couldn't remember what she'd been doing. She had a vague recollection of spending the previous morning staring out her bedroom window at the overcast Pittsburgh sky. She hadn't even noticed that many of the buildings across the street had been decorated for Christmas. This meant it was after Thanksgiving because the city always started decorating shortly after Black Friday. It was strange how she'd lost all sense of time since Derek had died. She guessed that it was her equilibrium betraying her. Her sense of balance had been knocked out of whack. For a moment she wondered if it would ever come back. The she realized she didn't care.

Christmas was Derek's favorite time of year. He loved walking down the snow-covered streets. Stopping at the brightly decorated window displays. Enjoying the endless holiday scenes. Laughing and acting like a little boy. His Christmas movie collection had been impressive. He owned more than a dozen different versions of *A Christmas Carol*, as well as more than thirty different Christmas movies produced by the Hallmark Channel. His collection was one of the first things he showed her when they started seeing one another. He kept the DVDs on the shelves of his bookcase in his Oakland apartment, along with his old movie collection and several shelves of hardback novels, mostly mysteries and suspense. His posters of *Casablanca*, *Citizen Kane*, *North by Northwest*, and *Psycho,* all professionally framed and matted, adorned the opposite wall.

But now, Christmas no longer seemed to matter. With Derek gone, the brightness had gone out like a snuffed-out candle. Her happiness had vanished completely, as with a wispy cloud in a thunderstorm. It hadn't even mattered to her that Dad and Mom had been, as always, adding their ornament collection to the living room and kitchen, placing their tiny Santa Claus statues carefully on the mantelpiece and living room shelves and putting their expensive Hallmark scenes on top of the kitchen cabinets. The few times she'd noticed them during the last week had forced her to turn away. To blot them from her mind. They'd somehow become just some dreaded distant memory. Some silly things she remembered from another life. For Paula, Christmas meant sharing it with Derek. Now that he was gone, Christmas had died as well.

She gently placed his photo face-down on the white laced doily on the wooden surface of her dresser. Then slipped on her housecoat, shoved her feet into her slippers and plodded over to the door.

For the next few minutes, she stared anxiously at the doorknob, contemplating it as if it were something frightening. Something that would cause her great harm. Something she dared not touch. *I have to open the door,* she told herself. *If I want coffee, I need to leave this room.*

But did she want to?

Did she really need coffee? Or was she just doing this to keep her parents from worrying?

Did she honestly think that opening the door and walking out into the hall would make things better? Would it improve anything at all? Would it bring Derek back?

For her, leaving the sanctuary of this room meant forcing herself out of her self-imposed seclusion. Rejoining the human race. Opening up the lines of communication again.

What exactly did the human race mean now? A life without Derek. A future without the love of her life. Being alone. Being miserable. Facing the rest of her existence without her soulmate.

But what choice did she have? Did she really want to venture outside? Or did she want to stay here and live out her existence in darkness, with only the memories of Derek to help coax her through life and into the next world?

Open the door, baby doll...

Derek's voice again.

Or was it her own?

It didn't matter. She had to do it. She couldn't stay here forever. That much she knew. *Baby steps,*

18

as Derek would say. *One foot in front of the other. You can do it. You're made of much tougher stuff than this. You'll do it and you'll make me proud...*

Yes. I have to make him proud. I can't just give up. I'm only thirty-two years old. Everything lies ahead of me.

Thirty-two years old. If she lived to the age of seventy, that meant she had more than half her life to live. Thirty-eight more years. Thirty-eight years without Derek. Without the love of her life beside her...

Thirty-eight years by herself...

I can't. I just can't! I'm just no good by myself—

You can do it, baby...

Can I? Can I really?

You can. I know you can. You have never been one to give up so easily.

Yes, my love, I have to. If I stay here much longer, I might as well just find Dad's gun and blow my brains out, right here and now...

That's out of the question, sweetheart. You're better than that. I didn't fall in love with someone who thinks so little of herself...

Taking a deep breath, she grasped the doorknob, flinching at its coldness. Then, after another deep breath, she gritted her teeth and pulled.

The bright yellow light of the hallway nearly blinded her. She closed her eyes and stood in the doorway, trembling while struggling to gather enough courage to force her legs to start moving.

C'mon, baby... Make me proud...

Taking one last deep breath, she squared her shoulders. Then, opening the door a couple of inches more, she stepped stiffly out into the hall.

Chapter 3

Mom and Dad sat at the kitchen table, sipping coffee and staring at one another. The kitchen smelled strongly of toast,
vanilla coffee, and bacon.

A flash of memory gave Paula pause the moment she stopped in the archway. A lifetime ago, she, Tricia, and Boyd scrambling from their bedrooms to chow down breakfast before bolting out the door. Then running down the stairs and reaching the end of the block just in time for the school bus to pick them up and take them off to school. Boyd always scurried to the back of the bus to be with his friends while Paula sat closer to the front, with one of her own classmates. Tricia usually sat with her friend Brittany, the cute blonde who wore costume jewelry, even in the first grade.

It was strange, thinking of those memories right now. It had all happened so long ago, in a different world.

Everything was different back then. Priorities remained constant: getting your homework done, staying away from the wrong crowd, making the right friends, and making sure you didn't set yourself up as a target for cyberbullying. Once school was out and the bus brought you back home, you felt safe.

Her room had always been her sanctuary. Her whole world consisted of her cell phone, notebook, books and movies, CD player, TV, clothes, and shoe collection. Tricia and Boyd spent time with her but had their own interests and were out on their own long before she realized it. Then she discovered she was alone and still had a few more years of childhood left.

She couldn't wait to grow up. To become a young woman. To be on her own, living in her own place. To be responsible to no one but herself. To make her own way, her own destiny. To be able to find someone she truly loved, who loved her right back. Someone she could talk to. Someone she could trust. Someone she could give herself totally to.

Someone she wanted to spend the rest of her life with…

Snapping back to painful reality, Paula shuffled into the room and went over to the coffeepot. She poured a cup, added sugar and a smidge of cream, turned, and went over to the table. As she sat facing the oven, Dad on her right and Mom on her left, she hoped they wouldn't force her to engage in awkward, mindless conversation.

"Toast, honey?" Mom picked up the plate and held it out for her.

"No thanks, Mom."

"You're sure? You really haven't eaten anything in—"

"I'm sure, thanks."

Mom put the plate down.

Paula picked up her cup and sipped. It tasted heavenly. She quickly found that she already began feeling more alive.

Dad nibbled on some buttered toast and picked up a scoopful of scrambled egg with his fork. "Feeling any better this morning, baby?"

She couldn't believe he'd asked her something like that. *This isn't a cold*, she wanted to tell him. *It's not something I have to shake, and it's nothing that's ever going to go away. My life was just torn apart by its roots. The love of my life was taken from me, my heart yanked out and ripped into so many pieces, it'll take the rest of my life to find what's left of them and put them back together.*

She just said, "Good coffee, Mom," and hoped she wouldn't have to reply to her father's ridiculous question.

Dad began staring at her. She didn't know if it was because he suddenly realized what he'd just asked her or if he had something else he wanted to say. She just hoped it wouldn't be as heartless as his last question. She knew he wasn't deliberately trying to be unfeeling. He was just worried about her and dealing with it the way all fathers felt they should deal with such a personal tragedy. Since he had no idea how to handle this, he was totally clueless. But she knew he cared.

"Baby, I know you won't wanna here this, but—"

"Dad, I really don't want to talk, okay?"

Sighing deeply, he slipped the forkful of scrambled egg gently into his mouth and glanced at the wall clock.

Paula felt a pang of guilt. She hadn't meant to snap at either of them. She wanted to yell at herself for doing so. They meant well. She knew how difficult it was to talk to someone who'd just been through a horrendous experience. Just six months earlier, when her Aunt Mary lost Uncle George after forty-seven years of marriage, Paula discovered that talking to her had been just as difficult as trying to communicate with someone lying comatose in the hospital.

It's just like me. I'm walking around and going through the motions, but even so, I'm just as comatose as Aunt Mary was.

"I'm sorry," she said softly. "I'm just...I just can't do this. Not yet, anyway."

"Yes, dear," Mom said. "We understand."

After about a minute, Dad said, "Derek's folks called last night, baby."

She practically spilled her cup. It took her several tense moments to collect herself. She sat hunched over, staring at the napkin in her lap. Derek's parents. Yes. He had parents, too, and they were hurting just as much as she was. Possibly even more than she was, if that was humanly possible. After all, they'd brought Derek into the world, raised him and sent him off to school. Just like Paula's parents had done with her. Nurtured him. Laughed and cried with him. Shared his childhood memories. The whole nine yards.

They might even hurt just as much as I am.

It didn't seem possible, but she imagined she could be right.

The hole in my heart is probably no bigger than what they're lugging around.

I don't want to know what they said or why they called. I really don't. I can't. It won't help anything. It won't help at all…

But in spite of it all, she found her curiosity getting the better of her. "What did…what did they say?"

Neither Mom nor Dad replied.

"I guess they just wanted to know…how I'm doing."

Dad shook his head and stared at his plate. "Not just that, baby."

The way he was avoiding her gaze frightened her, told her something else was going on.

"What, then?"

"They did ask about you," Mom said softly.

Dad sighed deeply before he spoke. "We think…we think they'd really like to see you."

Paula stiffened in her chair.

They'd really like to see you…

The dreaded words echoed in her head, over and over.

There was no way she could face them. It was much too soon. Seeing them at the funeral, hugging them, staring into their tear-stained faces… It had been horrible. But at least she'd been able to hide behind her heavy black veil. They hadn't been able to see her tears, her trembling lips. The horror that had clearly taken over her features. And she'd forced her wet, swollen eyes tightly shut while standing near them. And after, as they left the church, Dad stood close by to hold her up when her balance suddenly evaporated just moments before she sensed the hard ground coming up to pull her

25

down. Dad was right there. So was Boyd. And William, Derek's older brother, as well. Their support had helped immensely. They'd even escorted her back to the limo, helping her get back in and driving her to the cemetery. And were right there to catch her when she'd collapsed while picking up that beautiful bouquet of cut flowers she'd wanted to drop onto Derek's casket.

But now would be much more difficult. If she chose to see them, she'd have no one to hold her up. She wouldn't want Mom and Dad with her. She wouldn't want anyone with her this time. She realized she'd have to do this by herself. That Derek's parents would want this to be a private visit. But this would mean that she'd have to drive to Derek's childhood home by herself and face them alone. There would be no excuse this time for weakness, for moments of sudden hysteria, blankness of mind or loss of balance. She'd be entirely on her own, facing the parents of the man she'd loved so very much. A man who'd been taken from all of them so savagely, many years too soon.

"Baby?" Mom was watching her. "Did you hear your father?"

"Yes..."

"Well? What do you think?"

"Did they actually...I mean, did they specifically ask to see me?"

"Well no," Dad said, "but—"

"Then how do you know what they want?"

Mom and Dad fell silent.

26

A moment later, Dad said, "We both could tell. We could hear it in their voices. Besides, we both think it would be nice if you made the effort."

"We think it would give you—and them—some sort of closure," Mom said.

Dad nodded. "Not now, of course. Later, maybe, when you start feeling more like yourself. A few weeks, perhaps. Or maybe a month. Then—"

"I really don't think I can... I can't possibly think about seeing them right now."

"Baby, I honestly think you need to at least consider it. As I said, it doesn't have to be now, but—"

"Dad..."

"They need to see you as well."

She shook her head. "I don't... I can't... I'm a mess right now."

"So are they," Mom said, her voice a broken whisper. "So are we."

"The healing has to start *some* time, baby."

She stood up shakily, pressing her palms onto the edge of the table for support. Her nerves had started shaking and sputtering again. She couldn't keep the trembling from traveling down to her knees and making them weak.

This was pathetic. She couldn't even stand up in her parents' kitchen. How could she possibly manage to make it to Derek's place without losing control of the car and killing herself in the process?

This coffee thing was obviously a bad idea. The last thing in the world she wanted was to have an argument with Mom and Dad. "I'm gonna go back to my room and lie down..."

Dad said, "Would you mind if we invited them here—maybe in a week or so—and—"

"No." She felt her blood turn to ice. "Please...*please* don't do this. I can't possibly think of making plans about anything. I wouldn't want them coming here. Not for a while. I wouldn't be able to stand it. I couldn't...I can't...I *won't see them!*"

"Why can't you at least consider it, Paulie?" Mom asked.

"I don't know. I can't.... What I'm trying to say is...I just can't face anyone right now..."

"You can't shut yourself off forever, dear."

"I know, Mom."

"One day, you're gonna find that you're all alone."

"I *feel* all alone now. I hope you can understand that."

Mom nodded. "But one day, honey, we're not gonna be here for you."

She didn't even want to think of that right now. "Hopefully, that day won't come for a long time."

"What about your career? Your job? Your future? You can't just turn your back on your life and lose yourself in some sort of—"

"I can't think about *any* of that right now. I'm sorry, but I really can't. I've been sitting in my room for weeks, and all I can think of is Derek, and what we once had, and what I just...what I just lost..."

"Paula," Dad said, "we can't just sit by and watch you fall apart like this. You've got to start living again, baby."

28

"Please...don't..."

The tears returned. The trembling made the room go all funny. She nearly lost her balance once again. She could feel the darkness thundering back and knew that if she didn't lie down very shortly, the ground would come up again and pull her right down.

"I'm *so* sorry," she muttered brokenly. "I really am. But I've got to...I need to...go back to my room and...and lie down..."

Moving stiffly, she shuffled back down the hall.

The tears flowed more freely the moment she lay down on the bed.

Sleep came quickly, releasing her once again from cold, harsh reality.

Chapter 4

When she awoke, the thick gray haze outside her window told her it was late at night or extremely early in the morning.

She rubbed her eyes. Once her vision cleared, she squinted at the digital clock on her bedside table. It said 2:37.

She had the strangest sensation that she wasn't alone. That someone else was in the room.

Suddenly tense, she turned on her left side and saw—or thought she saw—a hazy shape sitting in her chair, watching her.

Was it Derek? Or was this merely her imagination?

Was she still asleep? She had read something about distraught people hallucinating as they slept, thinking they were awake when they were still sleeping. Seeing things, imagining things. Things that really weren't there.

She knew she could definitely qualify as distraught. If losing the love of your life so suddenly and senselessly doesn't tear you up inside, fill you full of rage and make you more than ready for a few months in the rubber room with a steady regimen of hallucinogenic meds in your diet, you just weren't normal.

She slapped herself smartly on the cheek. *Stinging pain*. That alone made this much simpler. The body feels pain instantly when in a conscious state. To make sure, she rubbed her wrists together and immediately experienced the sudden warmth growing within them.

There. I'm definitely awake.

So why do I feel like I'm not alone?

Rubbing her eyes again, she squinted at the darkness. When an image failed to materialize, she sat up in bed.

"Is anyone…there?" Her voice was no more than a broken whisper.

Silence.

Then: *"Go see them…"*

She gasped. Had she heard a voice? Or was she hallucinating even though she was wide awake?

"I'm awake," she whispered, this time to convince herself. She patted her cheeks again, rubbed her wrists. *Pain. Warmth.* "Awake. Wide awake."

But if she really was awake, had she heard someone's voice? Had she seen someone sitting in her chair? Had she glimpsed an image? Or had it been remnants of a dream?

Was it a vision? A spirit?

Or was this just one of the many strange illusions she'd experienced in the long, agonizing weeks that followed her losing Derek?

Her lamp sat on the nightstand just a couple of feet on her right. All she had to do was reach over and flip it on. Then she could see for sure—

No. I don't want to do that. I can't. I don't want to fill this room with light and find myself gawking at an empty chair. That will convince me I'm hallucinating, and I don't want that. I don't want to think that I can no longer trust my eyes, my ears. Most of all, my mind.

Besides, the darkness felt much better. Softer. More manageable. She'd grown quite fond of the darkness during the last six weeks and found herself much more uncomfortable and agitated in the presence of harsh light.

I'm awake. I don't need light to prove that. I know something doesn't feel quite right, but that could be attributable to other things. I might have had a dream about this, for all I know. It's really no big deal. I need to come to my senses. I might have dreamed this, but I'm awake now, and there's no one else in the room with me.

What about the voice she thought she'd heard?

"I...don't know." She'd whispered it. She thought that if she heard her own voice, she might be able to think more clearly.

Or maybe she thought the vision—or spirit— might hear her and reply.

"Go see them. They need to see you. And you need to see them."

My God. She'd heard it again.

Was it Derek's voice? Or her own conscience?

Her conscience, most likely. She felt guilty for not wanting to see Derek's parents. Her mind was rebelling.

Yes. Her conscience. It had to be.

How could she possibly know, one way or the other?

She swallowed, took a breath. "Derek? Is that...is it you?" This time, she spoke just above a whisper. As she spoke, she focused her full attention on the empty chair.

Silence. Then she heard the voice again. It seemed to be coming from her mind.

"They need to see you, talk to you..."

She wrapped her arms around herself to keep the shivering down. The voice felt like it was in her mind. But it sounded so real... "I don't think I can," she told herself.

"You can, baby doll."

Baby doll... Only Derek called me that...

My God...

She closed her eyes, and a bright vision appeared in the darkness of her mind. It was Derek. He faced her, smiling, his handsome face becoming more and more distinct.

It was truly him. It was Derek. The life of her life...he had somehow returned.

Startled, she opened her eyes and scanned the darkness of the room.

She was alone.

Once again, she considered switching on the lamp. Her right arm unconsciously straightened, reaching for it.

No. What if she was truly alone in the room? The very thought of it was unbearable.

She let her arm drop.

"Derek?" She swallowed a warm lump in her throat. "Is that...is it really you? Are you really here with me?"

"You can do it. You must."

Again, the voice seemed to be coming from her mind.

33

She closed her eyes again. Darkness. Emptiness. Her pulse racing, she waited. And waited. His vision did not return. She opened her eyes and focused once again on the empty chair. Maybe if she spoke directly to it…

"But my parents…they'll never understand."

Silence.

Sighing, she kept on.

"I can't see anything good coming from this. I can't possibly face them. I can't look at them and see your eyes. Your face. Your smile."

Silence. Then:

"You have to do this. They need this, too."

Yes. She needed to do it. Despite everything she feared, everything she wanted to avoid, she knew what had to be done. And so did Derek's parents. She didn't want to, but deep down, she knew it was the right thing. And she had to do it alone.

"I guess I have to do this alone." She hoped that by saying it, she could talk herself out of it.

"Alone, baby doll."

She wondered when she should do it. The answer, once again, came from the inner depths of her mind.

"The sooner, the better."

Yes. It had to be done soon. Otherwise, she wouldn't be able to do it at all.

She closed her eyes once again. Although she still wasn't sure if it had been him communicating with her, she sensed an overwhelming need to tell him how much she loved him. How much she missed him.

34

"Derek, I love you…and I miss you…so very, very much."

Silence.

A moment later, she heard her inner voice once again. As before, she couldn't help wondering if it truly was Derek's voice. *"I know, baby doll. I know."*

"I love you *so* much…"

Silence.

She waited.

More silence.

Paula fell back onto the mattress. She closed her eyes.

The tears returned.

Chapter 5

It was just after 4:30 when she tiptoed down the dark hall and saw her father sitting in the semi-dark kitchen, a bottle of Scotch on the table in front of him, a glass in his hands.

Paula's pulse hastened at the sight. Dad didn't usually drink late at night. Normally he had a drink or two after dinner, while he and Mom were watching TV. He almost always mixed it with soda. She'd never seen him drink straight from the bottle.

This was obviously because of her. Dad never liked seeing her suffer and didn't handle the frustration very well—especially when he realized he couldn't do anything to help. Not so many years ago, he'd held her after she'd run home sobbing from falling and scraping her knee or elbow. She could still feel his strong arms around her, protecting her, making her feel safe and warm as Mom applied the mercurochrome and bandages. She would never forget how his harsh, low-pitched voice instantly turned soft and gentle when he leaned closer and whispered, "You're gonna make it, Paulie baby. It's just a scratch."

She wondered, for a moment, if she should ask if he was okay. She decided not to. She could tell he wasn't doing well at all. And if all it took to help him cope was a little Scotch, she decided that was perfectly fine with her.

"Dad?"

He studied her in silence, noting the charcoal-gray winter coat Derek had bought her for

Christmas last year, jeans, and leather boots. And when his inspection settled on her brown leather handbag, which she held with its thick leather strap resting on her left shoulder, and the small overnight bag she gripped in her right hand, his bleary-eyed gaze immediately returned to her face. "Little early in the mornin' to be goin' somewhere, girl…"

"Dad, I didn't want you to see me—"

"You're goin' to see his parents, aren'tcha?"

She sighed. "Yes, Dad…"

"Changed your mind, eh?"

She nodded.

"Why so damn early?"

She couldn't tell him that she thought Derek's spirit had visited her in her room. She couldn't tell him what she imagined the voice had told her. Or that she felt compelled to do this on her own. She couldn't possibly tell her father that she had to do this because the darkness that had taken over her spirit was slowly killing her. Or that she strongly felt that this was the only way she knew to make the darkness go away.

"I…don't know, Dad. I just…it's complicated… I don't even know if I fully understand what I'm doing. How can I expect you to?"

He lifted his glass and had a sip of Scotch. He was staring at the cabinet on her right, next to where the refrigerator hummed, moaned, and clicked. She didn't think he was drunk. She'd only seen him drunk once. A long time ago. It happened when his mother had died of cancer.

Dad had been very close to his mom. Watching her die a little each day, until she'd taken her last breath nearly eight months after her diagnosis, had taken quite a toll on him. He'd handled his grief the way he'd handled most everything else in life. Silently. Inwardly.

After Grandma's funeral, Dad had driven everyone home and hadn't said a word during the trip back to the apartment. Then, still silent, he'd collapsed on the couch, drank half a bottle of Scotch, lay back and slept for the next twenty-four hours. And said very little for the next couple of weeks.

"You can at least give me an idea," he said. "I might not understand, but I promise I'll try…"

She still didn't want to tell anyone what had happened in her bedroom. She was afraid Mom and Dad might think she'd had a bad dream. Or had been hallucinating. They'd want to take her to a doctor and wouldn't take no for an answer.

She didn't need a doctor. For one thing, she didn't think she'd dreamed any of that at all. Even if she had, she didn't think a doctor could do anything but prescribe a regimen of meds that would most likely make her physically ill.

"Like I said, I don't even know what I'm doing. I feel like I'm sleepwalking most of the time. I don't have any energy and don't want to do anything. Nothing seems to matter anymore. Does that make any sense at all to you?"

He put the glass back onto the table. "I think so…"

"Really?"

He shrugged a beefy shoulder. "Maybe…"

"Then maybe you can tell me what you think is happening to me."

He watched her for a few moments, his blood-shot eyes barely open. Then turned back to the cabinet. He didn't say a word. After a few moments, he gazed at his clasped hands on the table in front of him and seemed to shrink a little in his chair. He continued gazing at them as he spoke. "You're goin' through somethin' very bad, Paulie. It never shoulda happened in the first place, and it's somethin' no one should ever have to go through. But it did happen. You're stuck with it 'cause it happened to Derek. And when it happened to him, it also happened to you. And now you gotta struggle through it however you can and find your way out of it. There's prob'ly more than one way out, but you gotta find the best way yourself. And you gotta do it alone."

"Dad, I wish I could tell Mom about this. I don't really want to leave without…without telling her my plans, or that I feel so spacey and lost all the time…"

"Your mother knows what goin' on, believe me. But I'll tell her what you just told me. You just do what you gotta do, okay?"

She wondered for a moment if she should change her mind and tell him what she'd experienced in her room. She thought he just might understand. Then, as she watched him slowly lifting his glass again, she thought better of it.

His glazed expression told her the obvious. He probably wouldn't even remember what they'd talked about. And even if she did tell him about the voice, he probably wouldn't believe her. He'd think it might actually be hysteria brought on by her grief. That she had in fact fabricated whatever image, whatever inner voice, she thought she'd seen and heard. It was because of her loneliness. Her sorrow. Her broken heart trying its best to deal with all this.

When she thought of this, she realized that might have been what had really happened. Maybe it *was* her imagination. Her grief. Her loneliness. Her broken heart. She'd never before known such sorrow but imagined how powerful it could be when unleashed fully. What it could do to the mind. The heart. The spirit.

She told herself that it didn't really matter what had happened in her bedroom, or whether it *had* been Derek's spirit visiting her. The fact remained. She had to do this. If it had been her imagination, or maybe even her conscience, she must do whatever it took to rid herself of the darkness smothering her. She honestly felt that if she didn't fight this, it would eventually kill her.

She bent and planted a tender kiss on Dad's forehead. "I'll be back as soon as I can," she whispered close to his face.

He looked up at her. His eyes didn't seem as glazed as they'd appeared just moments ago. His voice was dead-steady. "Come back when you've done what you have to do, Paulie. And just remember, we're here whenever you need us. You have your cell. I can be wherever you need me just as fast as I can get there."

"I'll remember, Dad. And thanks."

He shook his head and sighed.

"What's wrong?"

"I just wish you weren't goin' right now."

"Why not?"

"There's an arctic storm comin' in. It's due to hit the Ohio Valley by this evening, or early tomorrow morning. I don't want you gettin' caught in it. At least you've got the snow tires on the Honda, right?"

"Derek..." She sighed. "He had them put on that last week before he...while I was at the bank." It was tough saying that. It brought back even more sadness. She swallowed and cleared her throat to force the tears back. "Besides, it's only a thirty-minute drive, normally. I'll take my time. I promise."

Dad didn't say anything. He placed his large hand over hers and squeezed gently. She could see that his eyes were wet as well. "Well, be careful anyway."

"Thanks, Dad." She gave him another kiss. Then pulled the strap of her bag higher onto her shoulder, shuffled out of the room, went down the hall and left the apartment.

Chapter 6

Deer Creek, the large rural area where Derek had spent his childhood, sat nestled amongst sprawling hills, woods, valleys and creeks just twelve miles north of the city.

As Paula took her Honda north on Route 8, signs of Christmas showed in the lights and display windows of the stores she'd passed. Once she'd left the city limits, the first signs of snow began tapping lightly against her windshield. Her dash clock said 5:08. It was still dark outside, but the falling snow, moving from the west at a 45-degree angle, gradually obscured her vision. She slowed down from 50 to 40, letting the more adventurous motorists pass while upping her wiper speed a notch.

She had only a few miles to go before reaching the Bakerstown turnoff. Once she got off the state road and turned onto Bakerstown-Culmerville Road, she hoped she'd have less of a problem with visibility. The country road, winding, hilly and treacherous in places, saw much less traffic. This would enable her to relax a bit and concentrate totally on her driving. If conditions worsened, she could pull over and onto one of the many available side roads and wait until the snow eased up. She didn't think she'd have too much of a problem. It would take quite a storm to escalate in the next ten or fifteen minutes to make driving conditions hazardous. And as Dad had said, the storm wasn't due to hit the Valley until much later on in the day.

However, an approaching winter storm seemed to be the least of her concerns. What worried her most of all was that she had no idea what to say to Derek's parents once she'd pulled into their drive, walked up to their front door, and rang the doorbell at such an early hour of the day. Since it would soon be Christmas Eve, the family would be gathered together to try and celebrate with William, Derek's older brother, and whatever other relatives had come over to share in the holiday. Since Derek's passing, she knew this would not be the ideal opportunity to celebrate. All his life, Derek had made arrangements to be with his parents to help decorate the tree and share their Christmas feast as well as enjoy being together. This year, the family might not even want a tree. Derek's permanent absence would make this an extremely sad, painful occasion.

So why was she driving there in the first place?

Was it because she imagined she'd been visited by Derek's spirit during the night? That she was convinced he'd told her to do this?

Was it her fear taking over? The fact that she was terrified that the darkness hovering around her would eventually swallow her up if she did not soon resolve this horror?

She knew full well that she shouldn't breathe a word of any of this to anyone, especially his family. It would not only freak them out, but it would also convince them that she'd lost her sanity and was ready for intensive therapy and heavy meds.

But what *could* she tell them?

What could she possibly say when they opened the door and saw her standing there?

Would she be able to say anything at all? Or would her mere presence shock them into a quivering mass of sorrow and incoherency?

Would her surprise visit be too much for them to bear?

Would it bring back too many cherished memories, reminding them of the horrible present?

Am I doing the right thing? she asked herself, again and again. *Or will this be the worst thing I could possibly do to these people?*

She forced herself to remember that this hadn't been her idea. Something had happened in her bedroom just a few hours ago that had convinced her to do this. It could have been a hallucination, for all she knew. But if it wasn't, what was it? Her inner voice? Or was it actually Derek's spirit urging her to make this trip?

Whatever it was, it had worked. She was on her way. And in just a few minutes, she'd be halfway to her destination. It would be much too late to turn around and drive back to Oakland. She should just accept her decision and try and make the best of what she'd planned to do.

At 5:35, she pulled off Route 8 at the Bakerstown turnoff, coasted through the small town, pulled into the deserted front lot of a boarded-up building and sat there, wondering what to do next.

Once again, she thought about turning around and driving back to Oakland. Was it too late? Would it be foolish to drive back home?

What could this trip possibly accomplish?

She sat there for the next twenty minutes, as the snow and the wind increased in intensity. Sat perfectly still, debating with herself. Trying to convince herself that the worst thing she could do was to visit Derek's family right now. Her presence would remind them that Derek was dead and she was still alive. That would not be a good thing. They'd always thought the world of her and had mentioned several times that Derek could not have made a better choice for a mate and partner. However, things had changed drastically, and she knew for a fact that even though Mom and Dad had said that Derek's parents had called and asked about her, she was probably the last person they would want to see standing on their doorstep the day before Christmas Eve.

They'll see him when they look at me. They'll remember his smile. How he held me, hugged me, whispered to me. How we both laughed together, held hands. How he snuck kisses to me on the living room couch when he thought no one was looking. They'll remember snippets of conversation. His plans. How he talked to his mother about me when they were in the kitchen, preparing dinner.

I'll bring it all back. I won't even have to do anything. All they have to do is see me standing there.

She couldn't do this to these people. She had to let them grieve alone. In their own way. And she couldn't expect them to do it while she was there to remind them Derek was dead.

Just as she was about to turn around, the words she'd heard in her bedroom earlier that morning filled her head.

"Go see them. They need to see you. And you need to see them."

Yes. Even though she couldn't be one hundred percent certain what had happened in her bedroom, she strongly sensed that the inner voice she kept hearing belonged to Derek, and that they were his words that had filled her mind.

"All right, sweetie," she mumbled, wiping away the wetness gathering in her eyes. "Whatever you say. Right or wrong, we'll do this your way."

Then she pulled out onto the main street and headed east, on the two-lane road that would take her to Derek's childhood home in just fifteen minutes.

***

At 6:15, there was no traffic.

It was Sunday morning. Very few people would be driving to work. And since most church services generally started at eight or nine o'clock, the churchgoers would still be sleeping.

As Paula drove, the sky grew darker. The snow flurries increased in both size and intensity. The inside of the Honda grew much colder. She turned up her heater a couple of notches, increased her wiper blade speed and slowed her pace from 40 to 35. She'd been on this road a couple of times before, when Derek had brought her here to visit his family. Although it had been months since that last visit, she clearly remembered that their place was only ten minutes or so from Bakerstown. There

46

were no major turnoffs. Once she'd crossed the intersection of Bakerstown-Culmerville and Deer Creek Road, she'd have only another mile to go before turning onto the narrow one-lane gravel drive that would take her directly to the Manning house.

By 6:25, it had gotten even colder. Soon the wipers were unable to handle the heavy load as the snow activity increased dramatically. She slowed down to 25 and upped the heater another notch. Thank God she'd just had the Honda serviced. The heater inspected, the antifreeze replaced, the engine tuned up, the fluids replaced. She didn't need car trouble in any form this morning.

Keeping her left hand firmly gripping the wheel, she carefully pulled up the collar of her coat with her right hand to keep the back of her neck from getting cold. Then closed the front to protect her throat from the growing chill in the air. Although visibility had worsened, she hoped and prayed that her headlights would make it easy for oncoming traffic to see her.

However, that had never been an issue. There *wasn't* any other traffic. For one frightening moment, she came to the startling realization that she could be the only driver on the road.

Was her imagination taking over again?

True, it was very early, but she should be seeing *some* activity on the road. While this seemed sound reasoning, she remembered that she hadn't encountered any other vehicle on this stretch since she'd turned off Route 8.

Was it her imagination? Or was she letting her fears take over?

47

Fear or no fear, I'm all by myself. The growing horror began crawling heavily up her spine. *I'm all alone, and since the love of my life was recently taken from me, I'm not myself. I'm seeing things, hearing things and imagining things. There's an arctic storm developing out there. Dad said it wasn't due to hit quite yet, but for some mysterious reason, I seem to be caught right in the middle of it. Why shouldn't I be imagining all sorts of frightening things right now?*

After more serious thought, she decided to occupy her mind with something that would keep the panic at arm's length. She didn't need panic right now. She needed to stay calm. To keep a clear head. For that, she should work on some sort of strategy when she arrived at the Manning house. She couldn't just walk up to their front door and stand there, her mind totally blank while she waited for someone to answer the door. They'd think she'd turned into a zombie. Or that something horrible had happened to her.

Hello…I was just in the neighborhood, and—

That was probably the most ridiculous line she could think of. She had to be an idiot for even thinking something that lame.

Hi. I thought I should stop by and—

And what? Drop in and celebrate Christmas with Derek's family? Act like nothing out of the ordinary had happened? That Derek hadn't really died? That they should talk about him as if he was due to show at any minute? Or that his death meant nothing? After all, it was Christmas, and despite everything that had happened, everyone should just

48

forget about minor disturbances and setbacks and dip heartily into that eggnog, tear open the gifts under the tree, and sing those Christmas carols.

That was even stupider than her first idea.

She had to stop thinking of something that would sound feasible and just play it by ear. The truth, perhaps? It might not be as lame as it sounded.

I wanted to come out and see if I could possibly spend a few hours with you because I really and truly believe Derek would want me to do this...

That felt all right. The more she thought about it, the better it sounded.

They'd want the truth, wouldn't they? They wouldn't want to hear just anything. They wouldn't want to listen to something that would benefit her, but not them. They definitely wouldn't go for something that sounded dishonest and rehearsed. They were very nice, respectable people. They were also intelligent. Derek's father was a professional carpenter, his mother a former high school teacher. They'd be able to weed out the lies and take whatever she'd said from that point on with a grain of salt.

Derek, she thought as the sky grew even darker, *I'll make you proud of me. I'll tell your parents the truth, and I won't change anything just to make myself look better.*

Just as she passed the intersection of Bakerstown-Culmerville Road and Deer Creek Road, the sky grew black, and an inch of fresh snow covered the windshield. She slowed down to 15 as she went down the hill and around the horseshoe bend that Derek had warned her about several times.

"Dozens of people have misjudged this bend," he'd told her during her first visit to his home. "Most of them ended up in the ditch, or halfway down the hill. Some even died when they swerved into the other lane and slammed head-on into oncoming traffic."

The moment she cleared the bend, a large patch of black ice appeared in her lane. The Honda skidded over it, snow tires and all, and abruptly slid off the road sideways. A hill appeared on the right, a small grove of trees, and a length of guard rail disappeared to accommodate a wide, twisting driveway veering off sharply to the right. She pulled her foot off the gas pedal, but even then she knew it was too late. The cold intensified. More ice showed up on the ground just off the shoulder of the road surface. The Honda hit a bump. Then it began to slide sideways down the hill and fishtailed.

Everything immediately shifted. The Honda spun around quickly, and her sense of equilibrium vanished. She had the sensation that she was spinning, but since the snow had covered the windshield and the other windows, she couldn't see what was going on. She struggled to fight down the panic and forced herself to keep her mind working. Then, judging which direction she might be going, she tried righting the spun by turning the wheel in the opposite direction.

It turned out to be the worst possible decision. Instead of correcting the spin, the vehicle bucked and continued sliding down the hill. Panic finally took hold. She discovered that her hands had turned numb as they gripped the wheel. The moment she opened her mouth to get a good scream going, the Honda slammed into something hard and began sliding backward. She wanted to up the wiper speed to full so she could see what was happening, but she couldn't pry her hands from the wheel. As she forced herself to gawk stupidly at the windshield, she discovered that it was covered with a thick blanket of ice and fresh snow.

The realization hit her with the force of a sledgehammer. *When did all this snow suddenly turn into ice?*

Another wave of cold panic scraped heavily up her spine.

As the Honda continued sliding backward, it hit something solid and stopped abruptly. Something hard slapped her on the back of the head. Consciousness slipped away quickly as the darkness swallowed her up.

Chapter 7

Haze...

Then...a blur moving toward her...

A boy's voice. "Can ya hear me, lady? Lady? You okay?"

Feeling a heavy swirl of cold wind rippling through her, Paula shivered and opened her eyes.

A handsome young boy around twelve or thirteen stood just two feet away, staring at her. His wide-open dark-brown eyes told her he was very concerned. Almost scared. She could smell something sweet in his dark-brown hair and on his breath.

The throbbing in the back of her head made her wince. Her right arm weighed a ton, but she managed to reach up. She felt a gooey lump back there, just below the crown of her head. When she lowered her hand, she saw that her fingers were pitted with blood. My God. She shuddered and felt some warm dizziness coming back in fluttering waves. She closed her eyes and took a deep breath. *I can deal with this. I just bumped my head. I have a hard head. It's really no big deal. I just had some sort of accident. But at least I'm still alive and still able to move around. It could've been much worse.*

A moment later, the dizziness drifted softly away. "I think I just...I just hit my head..."

"Lemme help." The boy reached in and unfastened her seat belt. She tried helping, but another wave of warm dizziness made her weak, and all she could do was sit back and close her eyes

52

again. "It's all right," the boy said. "I'll take good care of ya."

She kept her eyes shut and tried to relax, to ride out the pain making the back of her head tingle. Just then, the pressure of the seat belt pressing against her loosened slightly. A few moments later, it vanished completely. She opened her eyes just as he carefully took her right arm. Then he pulled. Gently at first, then more firmly. She let him pull her and soon felt herself sliding out of her seat.

"Let me try… I want to… I have to stand," she said, her voice suddenly weak.

The dizziness came right back. Despite her efforts, she was forced once again to let the boy take over. He draped her right arm over his shoulders and grasped her wrist to support her weight. Her vision was blurry, but she could tell the boy was nearly as tall as she was. This was good. It made it easier for him to help walk her through the tall snow.

Tall snow…

Funny. She didn't remember it snowing so much. As she struggled to get her bearings, she recalled it snowing only lightly until she'd pulled off the state road. But as they trudged up the steep rise leading to the main road, she noticed that the snow was knee-high. Judging by its hardness, she decided that it had been lying here quite a while.

How long was I out?

How long was I sitting in my car?

After another minute or so of trudging through the deep snow, they climbed up the snow-packed rise to reach the road. Still supporting her, the boy dug into his coat pocket with his free hand and pulled something out. A moment later, a bright flashlight beam lit the way straight ahead, where the ice-covered road led down a steep hill.

Two figures had appeared near the bottom of the hill. Just behind them, a cluster of mailboxes stood on posts on the other side of the road. One figure was a man, the other another boy. They both wore ski caps, heavy coats, gloves, and black boots. As they drew closer, Paula squinted and reached up to wipe the fresh snow from her eyes. The figures gradually became clearer. The man looked vaguely familiar, the boy a younger version of the lad helping her down the road. The boy also looked familiar. He seemed to be about eight or nine.

The moment they saw her, they hastened their pace. The boy nearly slipped on the icy surface of the road. The man grabbed the boy's upper arm to prevent him from falling. Once the boy had regained his balance, the two managed to make it the rest of the way without incident.

"What happened, Bill?" the man asked. "She slip on the ice?"

"Her car's up there, Dad." The boy turned to his right and pointed with a gloved hand. "Looks like it spun, just missed the guard rail and slipped down the hill."

"Is it in the creek?" asked the other boy.

"Just a coupla feet short," the first boy said. "It'll need a tow."

"We'll look after that later," the father said, "once this storm passes." He approached her and studied her. He examined her eyes and seemed to be checking her out for a concussion. "Can ya hear me, Miss?"

She nodded.

"How bad ya hurt?"

She tried lifting her arm. "I think I hit my head…on something hard. Probably the door…or the head rest…"

The man moved closer. She detected a faint scent of beer on his breath. Although she couldn't see what he was doing, she sensed that he was checking her for cuts and bruises. He pulled back and smiled. Once again, she couldn't help thinking how familiar he looked. "It's not bad," he said. "Just a light tap. There's a little blood. We'll get ya fixed up in no time. Is there any place ya need to be right now?"

She struggled to remember but couldn't. Everything seemed hazy, unfocused. All that registered was that she'd come here for a specific reason. But right now, she couldn't quite pin it down. She just shrugged.

"Ya can't do much in this storm, so we'll take care of ya."

"Thank you…so much…"

"No trouble. If a body can't help someone on Christmas Eve, how can we possibly call ourselves civilized?"

Her head throbbed again. Was it Christmas Eve? Why did this seem odd to her? She took a breath and let them help her carefully and slowly down the ice-covered hill.

"Rick," the man said, "go tell your mother we're havin' a guest for dinner."

"Sure, Dad." The boy smiled at her before turning around and making his way carefully toward the one-story house in the distance.

That smile… It was so…so incredibly familiar…

"Rick?" she asked softly.

"His name's Derek," the father said.

"He doesn't like it much," the other boy said.

"Not yet," the father said, chuckling. "Once he's grown, he'll get used to it. It's a good name. Was my father's name."

Her pulse thundered. She began feeling weak again.

"*D-Derek?*" she said in a tiny voice.

"We're the Manning's, Miss," the father said.

Derek?

A boy?

Oh my dear God…

The throbbing had become a light hum that felt strangely comforting. She closed her eyes and surrendered to the warm haze filling her head.

56

Chapter 8

Paula awoke in a strange dark room.

The moment she sat up, the back of her head began throbbing. She reached up. With a shaky hand, gingerly touched a large bandage covering what felt like a lump at the crown of her head. Exhausted from the effort, she let her arm drop to her side. Then lay back down. For several long, frightening moments, she struggled to recall what happened and where she was.

Nothing would come. Her memories were all hazy and made no sense. The dark room and its unfamiliar bed didn't help. All she really knew was that this was not her room, and she was not in her family's Oakland apartment. But if this wasn't her room, where *was* she?

Then, during her confusion, the strange dream came back.

Rick.

His name's Derek... He doesn't like it much...

My Lord...

What on earth is going on?

She pushed herself up, brought her legs over to the edge of the mattress and let them dangle. The dizziness came back. She closed her eyes and sat forward. A dream. This had to be a dream. A weird, frightening dream. Nothing else made any sense.

Once the dizziness subsided, she opened her eyes. Even in the dark she could tell she was wearing her own clothes. Although her memories seemed to be in an advanced state of total mayhem,

57

she clearly recalled putting on this outfit not too long ago. Two, maybe three hours earlier? In her own bedroom?

She wasn't quite sure.

Forcing her mind on other things, she sat staring at the darkness, trying to sort it all out.

It was the strangest dream she'd ever had. She'd seen Derek...and his brother Bill...and their father...and...and...

They were *boys*. Bill and Derek were little *boys*.

But were they? Were they really?

Or had she just imagined it?

Put it together. Start from where you think this all happened and get it going...

She'd skidded off the road and bumped her head. A bandage now covered the wound. This suggested the possibility of a concussion. It also suggested someone had tended to her wound.

All right...so someone tended to the bump on the back of your head and placed a bandage over it.

Then what?

She'd woken up. This told her she'd been unconscious for quite a while. During her unconscious state, delirium had most likely taken over. And since Derek and his family had been foremost in her mind, it was only natural that they'd appeared to her among the confusion. And that they'd appeared at a much happier time in their lives. Years before Derek would grow into the man she would fall in love with...then lose in a single act of random violence.

That was it, then. Confusion. Delirium. Hallucinating. Her imagination taking over.

She continued staring at the darkness, her thoughts going back, recreating what had just happened. Considering. Then doubting.

Something about all this just didn't make any sense.

What had just happened…it wasn't a dream. It didn't *feel* like a dream. Not at all. It was too vivid. Too real.

No. She hadn't imagined it. Then what had just happened?

She'd somehow gone back in time. It could have actually started out as a dream, but that wasn't the end of it. It just wasn't the full story. She'd somehow gone back. She must have gone back twenty—no, thirty—years.

And then?

What about the trip? The drive from Oakland?

The moment a few important details came flickering back, she also recalled Derek's presence in her bedroom, hearing his voice in her head, which told her to—

To what?

She caught something out of the corner of her eye. Squinting, she made out a lamp on the bedside table just a couple of feet on her right. Even in the dark it looked strange. Unfamiliar. She was certain she'd never seen it before.

With a trembling hand, she reached over. Then, working by feel, flicked on the light underneath the shade.

The sudden brightness cast a golden haze on the unfamiliar room.

"This isn't my room..."

But she'd already known that, hadn't she? Of course she had. You knew immediately when you were in an unfamiliar room. The smell gave it all away. The feeling of discomfort. Of strangeness.

Suddenly nervous, she scanned the room. It was obviously a spare bedroom, with a couple of small landscape prints covering the wall facing her. A cedar chest sat beneath the room's only window. A heavy blanket of snow lay in a thick, wavy drift at the bottom of the windowpane against the darkness of the night.

"Where am I?" she whispered to herself. "What place is this? How did I get here?"

Now more curious than frightened, she pushed herself to her feet. A warm wash of dizziness overtook her. She sat back down, closed her eyes and rode it out.

About a minute later, she tried again, this time with some success. Her handbag and overnight case rested neatly on a rather old-looking cedar chest at the foot of the bed. She shuffled over to it. She was about to open the overnight case when she suddenly heard music coming from another room.

Christmas music. It sounded like it was coming from a stereo. The song, "*Joy to the World,*" drifted happily past the door.

Then she heard laughter.

Despite the laughter and the joyous holiday music, she sensed a terror building up inside her.

Then, in the midst of her rising fears, someone knocked lightly on the door.

Her heart thrashing, she backed up until her thighs pressed against the side of the bed. Her hands covered her mouth as she stared at the door, not knowing what to do. Should she open it? Who was out there? What would happen if she didn't open the door? Couldn't she just stay right here until she figured out what was going on?

But could she find out what was going on without opening the door?

Was it possible for her to figure this out all by herself?

What if the person knocking was the same person who'd tended to her and brought her in here?

Her mind reeled, the cascading images bringing about another wave of dizziness. She thought of Derek and Bill and their father. Then reached up once again to make sure she hadn't imagined the bandage on the back of her head. It was still there. Then she wondered why it was there and how badly she'd injured herself.

She remembered once again that she'd been unconscious. She'd been through an ordeal and had hit her head. That might have made her delirious. If so, she might have been hallucinating.

Had the blow to her head caused all this?

Was it still causing all this?

A flickering image of an icy road and her car sliding sideways showed briefly before fading. Then the strange voice she'd heard just hours ago in her bedroom flared up again.

The dizziness trickled back. Before she realized it, she began falling, surrendering to the approaching abyss…

Something soft pressed against her back just as the blackness swallowed her up again.

Chapter 9

When she awoke again, she experienced a heavy sensation of warm dampness covering the upper part of her face. Then she discovered that a washcloth had been placed on her forehead.

A pretty, red-haired lady around her own age sat on the edge of the bed, smiling at her. She was slender and long-limbed and wore blue jeans and a heavy light-blue sweatshirt covered with large white snowflakes. Her long hair was pulled back and tied in a thick ponytail. A silver necklace encircled her neck. If it hadn't been for the hazy golden light of the lamp causing the necklace to glitter, the silvery gems would have been lost among the snowflakes.

Paula couldn't help thinking that she'd seen this woman before. The large light-blue eyes. That smile.

In a soft, low-pitched voice, the woman said, "I see we're awake. You've been having an awful day, young lady."

"Wh-Where am I? Who are you?"

"You're in Gibsonia, honey. I'm Julie. Julie Manning."

Julie Manning. Derek's mother.

And she's my age...

My God... This couldn't possibly be happening!

Paula's entire body went numb. A strange tingling sensation began somewhere in the pit of her stomach. She had to tell this lady that something was wrong. This just wasn't the way things were

63

supposed to be. Something had gone seriously berserk in the great scheme of things.

"Ma'am, I don't know what's happening. This isn't right. I'm not really…this can't possibly be—"

"Please call me Julie."

Her pulse raced. Could this sweet young woman actually be Derek's mother? Could any of this really be happening?

Just how hard was I hit on the back of my head?

"J-Julie? Really?"

"Yes, dear. And what should we call you?"

She wondered for a moment what would happen when she told this woman who she was. Would this strange dream end once she'd heard Paula's name? Would everything just vanish? Would the woman freak? Would the room disappear and suddenly be replaced by Paula's bedroom? Would Paula wake up?

When I wake up, what will happen then?

Will I awaken on my bed? Or in my chair, with Derek's picture still pressed against my bosom?

There was only one way of finding out.

"I-I'm Paula." Her voice had suddenly become weak, unsteady. "Paula Hodgins."

"Nice to meet you, Paula." Julie Manning didn't flinch. It was as if she'd never heard the name before.

This made no sense. None whatsoever. None of this did. But what frightened and confused her more than anything else was the fact that this felt so *real*…

Was this a dream *at all*?

Or had something happened that defied any logical explanation?

"Are you feeling better, Paula? I knocked on your door about fifteen minutes ago. I didn't hear anything, so I decided to come on in and see about you. I hope you didn't mind. I just had to see if you were all right." Julie Manning shrugged. "Here you were, sprawled crossways on the bed. Did you faint?"

"I think I might have, yes…"

"Well then, we'll take extra special care of you right here, until the storm passes. It's a bad one, so it might last a couple of days. With these hills, it could take twenty-four hours before the snow trucks make it here to clear the roads. But once the storm passes, I'll have Brian take you in to see the doctor just to make sure you're all right, and that the bump on your head isn't anything to worry about. Does that sound okay with you?"

"I really don't want to be a bother…"

Julie smiled, shook her head and patted Paula's hand. "It's no bother, honey. If we can't help someone in need—especially on Christmas Eve— we can't call ourselves good Christians—or even good human beings. Can we?"

"This is so very nice of you…"

"It's no trouble." She stood up. Paula instantly saw that the woman was tall—possibly five-eight or so. But that was no mystery, was it? She'd seen Derek's parents many times before, and both were tall. Why should anything be different now?

But this woman is clearly my age, she thought, her pulse hammering. *She's in her mid-sixties, but*

*right now she's no more than thirty-five years old!
This makes no sense. This makes absolutely no
sense whatsoever!*

"How do you feel?" Julie Manning asked. "Any
better?"

Paula had to take a breath and force herself to
calm down. To forget about what she thought had
happened and concentrate on the here and now.
"Well, a little better, actually…"

"Good enough to join us out in the living room?
We've just brought out the tree. If you're up to it,
maybe you'd like to help us decorate it. But if
you're not feeling your best, you can just watch, all
right?" She lowered her voice. "Between you and
me, I'd want to stay clear and just watch. Those
boys of mine…" She shook her head. "Sometimes
they can be a handful. And my husband Brian is no
better." She shrugged. "You've heard the saying
about the apple that doesn't fall far from the tree?"
She smiled sheepishly and winked. "We really don't
wanna get in their way."

"I think I'd like to come out anyway. It'll make
me feel better."

"Good." She backed up and turned to the door.
"Well, all your things are here." She gestured to the
cedar chest at the foot of the bed. "If you'd like to
freshen up, the bathroom's right across the hall."

"I think I will, thanks."

"If you don't mind my asking, where were you
going when the storm hit?"

Paula stiffened. Her mind instantly looped with
all sorts of insane images.

66

Tell her the truth. If this is really happening the way you think it is, the truth won't matter either way, will it?

She remembered an old *Twilight Zone* episode with the same premise. How the main character proved the present situation was not real when he suddenly reached out and stuck his arm in the path of a working plane propeller. The next moment, the plane and everything in the dream vanished, with reality returning in the blinking of an eye.

She cleared her throat. And realized right then that she could not possibly tell this woman that she was coming here to see them. Or why.

"I was coming to see...to see some friends."

"Do they live out here? Maybe we know them. We could call and let them know you're safe. That is, if the lines aren't down. But in a storm like this..." She shrugged.

"It's all right." Paula pulled the washcloth off her forehead and forced herself to sit up. "I'll take care of all that later on."

Chapter 10

The living room rang brightly with the Christmas spirit.

An instrumental version of "*Deck the Halls*" played majestically from the stereo system on the shelf behind the TV set. A large Christmas tree box sat opened on the floor in the center of the room. Several boxes of ornaments, wreaths, tinsel and endless strings of lights were strewn onto armchairs, the back of the couch, the cocktail table, and both end tables.

Derek and his brother Bill sat on the floor in the middle of the room, untangling tinsel and garlands and removing ornaments from their boxes. Their father stood in front of the large living room window, carefully dragging a round table away from the center to make room for the tree while whistling along to the music.

Paula couldn't take her eyes off Derek, who was struggling with a thick tangle of garland he'd pulled from a box. He looked so vulnerable, so adorable. She could easily see shades of the young man he'd eventually grow into. The man she'd fall deeply in love with. The man who would capture her heart as well as her spirit just two or three decades from now—

No. This is all wrong.

This can't be happening!

Have I gone stark-raving mad? How in heaven's name can I think for even a moment that something like this has actually happened? How can I think that the little boy I'm watching right now is the man I loved, worshipped, and adored? The same man who was taken from me six weeks ago?

It was impossible to go back in time. Despite all the time-travel movies that had been made, the weird sci-fi TV shows that had centered around such a theme, she had read and learned from numerous sources that time travel was impossible. Despite technology, despite all the greatest innovations and advances in modern travel made by the world's greatest minds, no one could go back in time.

Yet, this certainly seemed like she had actually done just that. The furniture. The wallpaper. The rug. The ornaments. The boys themselves. Their parents. Everything suggested that she had gone back in time and had ended up somewhere in the mid-eighties.

She looked down at herself. For some strange reason, she was just as she'd always been: thirty-two-year-old Paula Hodgins, five-feet-four and a hundred and fifteen pounds. The same person who had graduated from the University of Pittsburgh ten years ago. The same person who, for the last eighteen months, had been chief teller at the First National Bank on Penn Avenue. The same person who was now standing in the living room of a family who would not even see the new Millennium for the next couple of decades.

What on earth had happened?

Had the bump on her head done all this? Had her concussion scrambled her brains?

The accident with her Honda?

The ice storm?

Or had she somehow stumbled into one of those inexplicable planes she'd read about in sci-fi novels years ago, in high school?

"I'm sorry, honey. I didn't know you were standing there." Julie came out of the kitchen, wiping her hands with a towel.

Turning, Paula noticed the small calendar hanging by a thumbtack on the pegboard inside the kitchen doorway. The moment she glimpsed it, her entire body turned cold.

December 1987.

She soon found that she couldn't take her eyes off of it.

1987. Not 2017, but 1987.

Thirty years. My God.

I should be two years old--not thirty-two...

There had to be some sort of logical explanation for this. The bump on her head had obviously done something to her. It had somehow caused her to fall into some sort of hallucinogenic trance.

The mere thought of this intensified her numbness, making her light-headed. She could tell the dizziness was already on its way and would soon take her away again.

Luckily, Julie's voice distracted her, snapping her out of her approaching dilemma. "Rick? Bill? Brian? This is Paula, and she's going to spend Christmas with us!"

The boys dropped what they were doing, got up and came over. So did Brian, who looked concerned. "You okay, girl? Ya look kinda pale."

70

"Brian, dear," Julie said gently, "can't you see that the girl's been through quite an ordeal? First, the storm, then the bump on her head. You told me her car slipped into the ditch, and she almost landed in the creek. She was very lucky she got away with just a bump on her head." She turned to Paula and shook her head. "Honestly, honey, I just can't believe what goes on in a man's head sometimes. It's like we're talking to an empty coconut most of the time!"

"I get it from my dad," Brian said with a chuckle.

"If you listened to him," Julie said flatly, "you'd think everything his father gave him had something to do with foolishness or downright hard-headedness."

"No comment," he replied with a chuckle. Then he grinned at Paula. "We're really glad you're gonna be spendin' your Christmas with us, little lady."

"Thank you." Paula could tell by his smile that he was sincere.

Brian winked. Then, turning, he went back to the box containing the tree.

"Hi," Derek said, smiling up at her.

Paula struggled to stay calm. *Just a dream*, she told herself. *I know it feels real, but it isn't. It can't be. None of this can be what it looks like. And you'll soon be waking up.* If she kept telling herself that, she hoped she might be able to get through this without freaking out.

"Hi." She noticed that he was kind of small for his age, the top of his head barely reaching the level of her mouth. But he still had quite a bit of growing to do, since he'd reached the height of just under six feet when she met him at her friend Sheila's Thanksgiving party in Oakland, where they quickly went off by themselves and found how much they had in common—

"You okay?" Derek asked.

Reality again. *Snap out of it, girl!*

"Pardon?"

He shrugged. "Ya look...sad..."

It was a struggle, but she somehow managed to force out a smile. "I'm fine, thanks."

"Dad'll get your car out tomorrow, once the storm passes."

"I know. I'm not worried."

He was still trying to untangle the string of garland and having trouble with a knot. "Where ya comin' from?"

"Pittsburgh." It was difficult talking to him without coming apart. She went right back and reminded herself that this was a dream. And like all dreams, this one would end. Then she'd wake up, most likely in her own bed, and see right off that things would be how they were supposed to be.

He smiled, and that tiny dimple in the corner of his mouth that she loved so much showed prominently. Right now, it seemed a little larger than she remembered. It would diminish a little in size as he got older and his cheeks grew fuller. "I'm gonna live there one day."

"You don't like it here?"

He frowned. "Everything's too far away."

"Like what?"

72

"The Pirates. The Steelers."

"He's *such* a baseball fan." Julie laughed.

"Football, too!" Derek tossed in quickly. Then he went right back to the center of the room, dropped to his knees and fought with the garland.

"Want some help?" Paula asked.

He shrugged.

She crossed the room, sat down facing him on the floor and took one end of the garland.

"Cool," he said, smiling.

"What's that?"

"You're okay. For a girl." He showed her his dimple again.

She found herself blushing. "What do you mean?"

"The girls I know don't like sittin' on the floor in their good clothes."

She couldn't help smiling. "I don't mind."

Derek nodded in satisfaction.

Bill chuckled. "Rick's got a crush! Rick's got a crush!"

Derek frowned. "My brother's nasty," he said, then stuck out his tongue at Bill. "Really and truly."

"He'll grow out of it," she said, feeling a tear beginning to form.

"Hope so. He embarrasses me sometimes."

"He'll be okay pretty soon," she said. "You'll see."

"You're not cryin', are ya?" he asked.

She blinked. "What makes you say that?"

"Your eye. It looks...wet."

"I'm fine." She wiped the tear away as quickly as she could. "I'm just having a good time." Then

73

she struggled to concentrate on untangling the garland for him.

Chapter 11

About an hour later, the tree was assembled and placed in front of the living room window. Covered with ornaments, blinking lights, tinsel and garland, its glittering magnificence filled the room with a glowing warmth.

As the Manning family stood in a semicircle smiling at it, Brian, balancing his lanky frame on a stepstool, made sure the angel sitting on top was level. Standing close to him, Julie adjusted the white laced skirting and added a few finishing touches to the tinsel on the uppermost branches. Kneeling off to the side, Bill gently shook one of the wrapped presents while Derek grew frustrated as he tried positioning a plastic snowflake in front of one of the lights to give it a bluish glow.

Paula went right over and helped steady the branch. Soon the snowflake was in the best position to reflect the light. As she stood close behind him, she took in his hair, his smell. The delicious closeness of him. She longed to touch him, to place her hands on his cheeks so she could turn his face toward her and kiss him. If only she could do it... If only her thoughts could change what was happening right now...

She closed her eyes, hoping with all her heart that when she opened them again, he would still be right there, close and touchable...but as a man. The handsome, wonderful guy she'd fallen in love with.

But when she opened her eyes, she saw that he was still the same eight-year-old boy he'd been only moments ago. Her heart sank. But even in spite of this, she felt herself weakening once again.

In her helplessness, she realized that she had unconsciously moved closer, until her face was just inches from the back of his head. Closing her eyes once again, she let her senses bathe in his presence. He might not yet be the man she'd once loved, but this was definitely Derek just as he was three decades before she'd met him. It made no sense, to be sure. And she knew that there was no logical explanation why this should be happening at all. But for some reason she could not begin to comprehend, it *was* happening. It *was* real. And whatever it was, it felt like it had become her true world.

She'd somehow escaped the other world. That cold, dark existence that had nearly destroyed her. This had most likely taken place directly after her road accident which, aided by her thoughts, her emotions and her sheer will, had enabled her to flee the cold terror of a forbidden dark place she never wanted to see again.

The other world was overwhelmed in bitterness and hatred. It was a disgusting, evil place, and took no prisoners. That world reeked of sadness, agony and death, and she was overjoyed that she'd managed to discover this strange, wonderful place. And as she bathed herself in the sweet innocence of the little boy standing in front of her, that same wonderful child who would eventually become the love of her life, she realized that she wanted no part of that other world.

She didn't know what or where this place was, but she did know that it was wonderful, and that she'd become part of it. And while she was here, she didn't have to worry about being sad or frustrated ever again. Derek was alive again. And through a series of bizarre, inexplicable events, she'd become part of his family again.

"Paula?"

Pulling herself out of her trancelike state, she turned.

Julie was standing right behind her, smiling at her. "Would you like something to eat, honey? I'm sure you must be hungry."

She smiled back at the sweet lady and suddenly realized that she was indeed hungry. She probably felt this way because she hadn't eaten in quite a while. She tried remembering when she'd eaten last, but since that minor detail had occurred in the other world, she decided that it didn't matter.

Nothing mattered in that other world. Nothing she wanted to think about, anyway. The only thing she truly cared about was that she'd gone back to a time in the past. A time when things were wonderful and nothing bad could ever happen. Time had stopped, and if she was lucky, it would stay this way.

She snuck another quick glance at Derek. Then turned back to Julie and smiled. "I really don't want to be a bother and have you fix anything special."

Julie shrugged. "It's no bother. It's dinnertime anyway. Besides, I made plenty."

Paula glanced at the large black starburst clock on the paneled wall next to the hall. It said 5:45.

"How long have I been here?" she asked, suddenly curious.

77

Julie shrugged. "I honestly don't remember, honey. I think they brought you here a little before seven this morning."

Seven o'clock. That meant she'd been here nearly eleven hours.

Eleven hours. It felt like fifteen minutes. The last thing she remembered putting in her stomach was half of a cup of coffee with Mom and Dad in the kitchen. But she couldn't remember how long ago that was. A day? A week?

How long had she been in her bedroom, sitting in the chair Derek had bought her, his photo pressed against her bosom, the tears staining her cheeks as she mourned his death?

I've lost all track of time…

"Something wrong, honey?" Julie asked, concerned. "You look… well, you look worried about something."

"I'm okay. And you're right. I really am hungry."

Julie smiled. "You'd better be. I made a roast."

"Smells great, babe." Brian sniffed and closed his eyes.

"You're in for a treat," Bill said. "Mom makes the best roast in the entire county!"

"Yummy!" Derek licked his lips.

Paula watched him, noting how his lips curled up. She remembered that he'd done that same thing when the two of them went to dine in some of the restaurants in Pittsburgh. He usually did that when their waitress brought them cheesecake. Or apple pie. Derek loved apple pie, especially with a blot of whipped cream sitting on top of it. In fact, he'd done that very same thing the last time they'd dined out. He'd had a large slice of strawberry cheesecake and had scarfed it down in no time. It was the day before—

Before that horrible afternoon, when Mr. Engel called her into his office and—

No. Don't even go there. Don't you dare go there ever again! This is a brand-new, wonderful, very special place, and there's no reason for sorrow, sadness, grief, or anything else--

It was at that moment that she noticed the delicious aromas drifting lazily from the kitchen.

Chapter 12

Dinner—a large pork roast, spinach soufflé, baked yams, corn muffins, buttered rolls, and a luscious dessert of freshly-baked apple pie—provided a symphony of succulence for the taste buds.

Paula couldn't remember the last time she'd enjoyed such a wonderful meal. Conversation with the family had also been a joy. Bill started talking about Little League, and the moment his father mentioned buying the two boys new bikes so they could ride to practice, Bill immediately reminded his parents that he'd be driving in just a few years.

"Four." Jagged rivulets of beer trickled down to Brian's chin when he jerked the bottle away from his face to provide his input. "Four years. Four!" He held up his free hand. Then, pushing his thumb out of range, he held up four fingers, which he shook forcibly at his older son.

"Three years and eight months," Bill corrected.

Julie joined in with laughter.

Reddening, Brian pulled in more beer. Then put his bottle down and went back to devouring the dark, juicy slice of pork he'd speared with his fork.

Derek just shook his head and stuffed half of a dinner roll into his mouth.

Paula noticed how Derek held his fork. She began thinking of that last dinner they'd had at Lombardi's, the popular Italian restaurant on Liberty Avenue they'd dined at on several occasions. They'd met one Friday evening after work and drove directly to the restaurant, where Derek knew the owner. They'd ordered ravioli and meatballs, and a good Chianti. The excellent wine had relaxed her and made the evening both unforgettable and dreamlike. The date had taken place about two weeks before…before…

Now is not the time to think of something like that. Not here. And certainly not now…

She knew she was right. This was not the time to entertain such dark, disturbing images. That horror had happened in the other world. The dark one she'd somehow managed to escape. In this strange new world, the little boy sitting next to her—that same wonderful lad who would later become the love of her life—was alive and happy and young again, and excited about Christmas and what he would see when he opened his presents the next morning.

"You sure do get quiet a lot."

Startled, she realized Derek was staring at her.

"A lot on my mind," she said, blushing.

"You'll find that a serious liability in this family." Brian sent her over a sly wink.

"Don't listen to him, sweetie." Julie glared at her husband. "This man gets quiet at the drop of a hat. And he does it in the wrong order. He's quiet when you want him to talk. Then he turns into a chatterbox when you want him to keep quiet."

"I may be a lot of things." Brian swallowed a forkful of yam and frowned. "A chatterbox just ain't there."

"You are so," Julie argued.

"Am not."

81

"Are so."

"Men aren't chatterboxes, babe."

"What's *your* word for it?"

He shrugged. "Maybe I get radical once in a while. Men can do that, ya know."

Julie tilted her head. "Are you saying women can't?"

"I refuse to reply to that." Brian picked up his beer.

"And why, might I ask, is that?"

"I've got my reasons."

Julie put her elbows on the table. "I'd like to hear them. In fact, I think we'd all like to hear them." She smiled at Paula. "How about it, Paula? Wouldn't you like to hear his reasons for this nonsense?"

Paula lowered her face and had a tiny forkful of spinach soufflé. "I don't think I'd better say anything to wear out my welcome," she said sheepishly.

"See there?" Julie shrugged.

"What are you talkin' about now?" Brian was still frowning. "The girl didn't say anything!"

"She's much too polite to agree with me with you sitting there," Julie said.

He sighed. "Want me to leave the room?"

Derek and Bill sunk down a little in their chairs.

"No, I want to hear your reason for refusing to answer the question."

"All right." Brian sat up in his chair and glanced at everyone. "I'll tell ya why I refuse."

"We're waiting…" Julie had a sip of her wine.

82

Brian took a breath. "I refuse to answer on the grounds that I really don't want to find myself sleeping alone on the couch on Christmas Eve."

Everyone laughed.

"Now…was that so hard?" Julie asked, the hint of a smile on her lips.

Brian scowled and tilted his beer. "A little."

"Seriously," Julie said, turning to Paula. "Tell us about yourself, Paula. Surely a pretty young thing like you has got a husband, or boyfriend."

The question startled her. Her mind reeled.

"I'm sure he's missing you right now," Julie added.

"Especially on Christmas Eve." Bill shoved a large piece of apple pie into his mouth, swallowing it whole.

Paula forced herself not to stare at Derek while struggling to think of something she could say that would sound reasonable.

Just then, Derek said, "Maybe she'd rather just spend Christmas with us." He gave her that bright expression she knew so well, his eyes sparkling, his mouth stretched into that delicious half-smile she'd loved so much. "You can call him tomorrow, can't ya? If the lines ain't down?"

"*Aren't* down," his mother corrected.

"Dad says ain't," he protested.

"Your father doesn't care what he says or how he speaks."

"I sure can't wait till *I'm* old enough not to care," Bill said, grinning.

"That'll be enough of that nonsense out of you, young man," Julie said sternly.

Bill reddened and quietly picked up his fork.

"Besides," Julie said, turning back to Brian, "it's too late for him to learn correct English. Or correct anything, for that matter."

"I resemble that remark." Brian feigned outrage.

"It's true, isn't it?" Julie countered, her brows arched.

Brian shrugged. "Maybe...but I still resemble that."

"When the lines *aren't* down," Derek said, watching Paula closely. "Then maybe you can call him?"

She felt herself weakening again. "Yes, Rick," she said in a soft voice. "I can do that. I'll try and call him tomorrow."

His little-boy's smile deepened, that tiny dimple making its typical brief appearance. She felt herself melting into a warm puddle. *I just don't know how much more of this I can take... But it's so wonderful, being with him again.*

But just as she began losing herself in this wonderful state of happy confusion, Brian said, "Tomorrow, after we open all the presents and have breakfast, I'll see if the lines are up. Jack's Garage is usually closed on the holidays, but he lives right behind the shop, and two of his sons live with him and Bernice. If I can get him on the phone, I'll ask him if he'll do me a big favor and send one of his boys down here with a truck. It's only a mile from here, so it's really no big deal. Besides, he owes me a coupla favors. After all, I did help him add on to that back porch when he couldn't get anyone else to

84

come over on such short notice. I've been a really good customer and friend the last ten years, so I don't think he'll quibble about taking an hour or so of his time for something like this, even if it *is* Christmas."

"No," Paula said quickly, "it's all right. Really." The thought of doing something— anything—that might end this wonderfully strange situation brought with it a sense of sheer panic. "I wouldn't want to impose on anyone else."

"Nonsense," he replied. "You're a guest, and we intend to help ya whatever way we can."

"It's not that we don't *want* you to stay with us longer," Julie said. "But we know you'd like to be on your way as soon as you're able to get your car in working condition again, right?"

The thoughts of leaving saddened her, but she knew she had to say something that wouldn't make her sound ungrateful, or suspicious. "Well, yes, but—"

"She can stay with us for supper tomorrow, can't she, Mom? Dad?" Derek looked anxious. Hopeful.

Paula had to force herself from letting go. Right now, the tears were more than ready to fill her eyes.

"Of course, honey," Julie said.

"But only if she doesn't have important business anywhere else," Brian said.

"Tomorrow's Christmas," Julie said. "I'm sure she doesn't have important business to tend to."

"What about family business?" Brian asked.

"I'm sure that will be something Paula will have to handle on her own."

85

"Well, she does have a call to make, doesn't she?" Brian turned to her. "You do, don'tcha, Paula?" he asked.

"Well, yes, I suppose so, but—"

"I knew it," he said. "A pretty lady like you probably has a nice young guy waiting for him somewhere, doesn't she?"

Before she could reply, Julie said, "He'd *have* to be really nice, wouldn't he, dear?"

Once again, she felt a heavy sense of warmth growing inside her as she smiled at Derek. "He is," she said. "He's the most wonderful man I ever met."

Derek smiled back at her.

She wondered if there was something behind that smile. It seemed innocent enough, but she couldn't help thinking that maybe he somehow knew what was going on.

You're being silly. How on earth could an eight-year-old know what was going on when you don't even know?

Still, that smile… It seemed almost freaky…

"Where's he work?" Brian asked. "Does he live around here?"

"He lived…lives…in Pittsburgh." Despite her efforts to keep it away, the other world drifted by dangerously close. Taunting her. Reminding her it was still there. That it hadn't forgotten about her. A chill trickled down her spine. "He's…he's an investment broker."

Derek frowned. "Bo-ring," he muttered.

"Not everyone can be an athlete." Bill picked up his last piece of apple pie and stuffed it in his mouth.

"Your guy," Derek said. "He ever play baseball?"

She stiffened. Once again, she felt disaster creeping closer, watching her, daring her to say the wrong thing. "When he was little. Maybe just a couple of years older than you are." She struggled to ignore the catch in her throat. "He loved it."

"What did he play?"

"Pardon?"

"He means, what position?" Bill washed down that last piece of pie with iced tea.

"I think he told me second base."

"That's what *I* play!" Derek practically jumped up in his seat.

"Finish your meal, young man," Julie said sternly. "You can continue with the acrobatics after we've finished supper!"

Chapter 13

Once supper ended, everyone, sated and comfortable from the excellent meal, settled into the living room.

Brian flicked on the TV. "*White Christmas,*" the 1954 holiday classic starring Bing Crosby and Danny Kaye, was playing on one of the local Pittsburgh channels. After adjusting the color on the screen, Brian sat on a small stool he'd placed in front of the fireplace and began roasting a tray of fresh chestnuts he and Julie had bought from the local supermarket. Bill and Derek sat on the floor, watching the movie while eyeing their presents scattered beneath the tree. Paula and Julie relaxed on the couch and enjoyed a glass of wine.

Paula had never experienced such a warm, wonderful Christmas. In the other world, she and her parents, along with Boyd and Tricia, had always enjoyed the holidays and made a special effort to be home for Christmas Eve to celebrate the next morning, unwrapping the presents and having breakfast. But even though everyone seemed happy and filled with the holiday spirit, Paula always sensed something missing, some special element of warmth that was very prominent here, with this family.

Tricia, who was two years older than Paula, preferred spending as much of her time as possible with her girlfriends. Boyd, the oldest, enjoyed having one or two of his friends over, as well. When the family was home for the holidays, Boyd normally had some college project to work on between his time visiting his old high school chums. Tricia usually spent most of her time on the phone with her friends, chattering away about school, boys, and the latest fashion trends. Dad very often had to work on Christmas Eve, or extremely early the day after Christmas. Most other times, Mom was exhausted from working long shifts the week before Christmas, and brought home Christmas dinner, which was prepared at the local market.

In this strange new world, everything was perfect—the tree, the lights, the magical warmth emanating from the fireplace, the pile of presents stacked beneath the tree. The family had come together and was obviously very happy and content being with one another. The wine, the roasting chestnuts, the snow tapping lightly on the living room window, the sparkling tree, the classic Christmas movie showing from the old-style television console... Everything fit together, like something out of Norman Rockwell.

I don't want this to end, she told herself over and over, as she watched Brian shaking the chestnuts on their tray. *I'm having a wonderful time. Derek is alive again. I just can't bear the thought of leaving this delightful family. I don't want to leave this world, either. I want to stay here forever.*

But even as her thoughts stayed bright and warm, a strange darkness kept drifting into the back of her mind, making her aware of the obvious.

This is too wonderful, too good...and you're much too happy and content.

Remember the saying: if it sounds too good to be true, it probably is...

She took a breath and pushed the forbidden thoughts aside. She couldn't do this. She just couldn't dismiss this perfect moment. She was here, enjoying all this. She had to stay here and make it last.

Don't think about those other thoughts. Not even for an instant. They didn't even exist. And they certainly didn't matter.

Toss the darkness away.

Her inner strength, gathering momentum, struggled to take over. To banish the forbidden thoughts from her mind forever.

There is entirely too much joy and happiness for you to enjoy and appreciate.

As long as you don't think of it, the other world will never be able to find you again.

Keep it away. It doesn't belong here. Make believe it's no more than an unpleasant intruder that will remain in darkness as long as you refuse to acknowledge its existence.

You've had unpleasant memories before—what was different here?

***

Before she realized it, the evening had ended, and she was lying in bed in the family's spare room, staring at the plastic candle lit up against the darkness of the night pressing softly against the window.

As she watched, she caught herself remembering when, as a child in the other world, she'd struggled to stay awake. Eagerly waiting to

90

hear the unmistakable sound of sleigh bells as Santa's sleigh and reindeer landed quietly on the roof. If she could stay awake, she might actually be able to hear everything. The sleigh landing on the roof. The bearded man himself climbing down from his seat. Picking up his bag. Walking over to the chimney. Slipping into it, sliding down into their living room...

Was it possible she'd returned to her childhood? Or was she being ridiculous?

You're a grown woman—do you still believe in such a thing?

The answer, surprisingly simple, came quickly.

I'm in a different world now. Derek is a little boy again. I've gone back thirty years in time. I'm spending Christmas Eve with his beautiful family, and I'm happier than I've been since Derek was taken from me.

How can I not believe in anything that has been happening to me in this delightful paradise?

Chapter 14

After a night of blissful sleep, Paula woke and hurriedly dressed.

The sun was shining brightly. Some of the ice had already melted on the outside of the windowpane, forming long icicles that twinkled as they dripped. She heard no more strong winds pushing against the house. The storm must have passed sometime during the night.

A feeling of sadness rocked through her. If the storm had passed, this would mean Brian would call his friend Jack and have someone drive down the hill from his garage, pull her car out of the ditch and tow it down to the house. Then, after it was inspected for damages, the Mannings would expect her to drive away and tend to her personal business.

She'd be forced to leave this beautiful family.

But where would she go? What would she do?

Why would she even *want* to leave?

She'd stumbled into this different world and found it wonderful. There was no sadness. No torment. No regrets. She hadn't been this happy since she and Derek were doing things together in the other world. She'd just spent the most joyous evening of her life with the nicest family she'd ever known and wanted it to go on forever. She was now deliriously happy. The heavy black shroud that had covered her from head to toe during the last six weeks had suddenly been lifted and permanently removed. Sorrow and agony had transformed into a slew of dark, distant memories that had vanished into oblivion the moment she'd escaped that cruel, dark world and entered this one.

I really want to stay here, she told herself. *I'm going to stay with these beautiful people in this stunning new world. The old world is gone and will never come back, so I won't have to worry about looking for a way of returning to it. If it can't find me, it won't know that I still exist. Maybe then it will leave me alone.*

But what about Dad? Mom?

Her job? Her career?

It didn't matter at all. She didn't even want to think about that other world. A world that had taken away the love of her life and threatened to destroy her by smothering her with darkness. She loved Dad and Mom. She also loved Boyd and Tricia, and had grown quite fond of the people she'd been working with at the bank. But even so, she knew that the only thing she truly wanted was to remain in this blissful new existence, where she could live forever in the past, with a family that loved one another and treated her as one of them.

What happens tomorrow? The next day?

She didn't want to think of that. She wanted only to concentrate on today—on now, this very instant—and whatever special miracles it held for her. After all, it was Christmas morning, and the Manning family was about to awaken from their slumber and celebrate the most wondrous day of the year. She wanted to be right there with them, in the middle of everything. She wanted to be sitting on the couch in the living room when Derek and Bill descended on their presents and opened them, sending the wrappings flying everywhere—just as she had done so many years ago, when she was a little girl. She wanted to watch the utter delight that would appear on their faces when they discovered what lay hidden in the boxes. The brightness in their eyes. The happiness. The sheer joy.

Then she heard activity down the hall.

It was no doubt Bill and Derek rushing into the living room to open their presents.

Oh my God, she thought, the panic causing her heart to pump rapidly. *They're already out there, opening their presents, and I'm still in here, visualizing what they're doing. I need to be out there with them, watching them rejoice on Christmas Morning.*

Containing the panic rising steadily within her, she hurried over to the door and opened it.

***

Derek was standing in the hall outside the kitchen doorway, his back to her. He was holding a coffee cup and talking to his mother.

Paula tiptoed down the hall. Her eyes stayed fixed on him. Something was different and very strange. Something her disoriented mind just couldn't grasp.

I'm still asleep, she told herself. *I've got sleep in my eyes. I'm not seeing this right. I need to rub the sleep out of my eyes. Then maybe I'll be able to understand just what in heaven's name is going on...*

Hearing her footsteps, Derek turned and smiled. Her pulse pounded when the realization ripped through her.

94

No longer an eight-year-old, Derek was now much older, and at least two inches taller than she was.

"Morning," he said in an older, low-pitched adolescent voice. "Merry Christmas!"

Just as a fresh batch of dizziness beckoned, she caught a shadow of movement slightly to her left, coming from the kitchen. It was Julie, and she, too, appeared different. Several years older, she looked at least ten pounds heavier than Paula remembered from the night before. She wore her red hair pulled back and tied. It had lightened somewhat, thinning a little just an inch or so above her forehead. She wore an apron over her long brown skirt and held a bright red oven mitt in her left hand. Her smile was just as bright as it was the night before but framed with several wrinkles around her eyes and near the corners of her mouth.

"Merry Christmas, young lady!" she said cheerfully. "And how'd you sleep last night?"

It took her long moments to find her voice. When she did, she discovered that it sounded a little choked. "V-Very well, thank you."

"Good. I just made a fresh batch of blueberry muffins. I hope you're hungry."

Not knowing what else to say, she heard herself mumble, "I think I am."

Grinning, Julie turned and went back into the kitchen.

Confused and a little frightened, she turned and glanced past Derek, at the tree in the living room. Presents had been placed beneath it, but not nearly the same number as she'd recalled from the night before.

Had they opened most of the others already?

If so, why would they leave half a dozen of them still wrapped under the tree? And where were the gifts that had already been opened?

She continued staring and suddenly realized that the tree was different. So were the lights. And the garlands. The tree itself appeared several inches shorter than the one she remembered from the previous night. She also noticed that there was no tinsel. The angel appeared to be the same, but slightly tilted. Also, it didn't seem as bright, but its halo had dropped a little, and the tip of one of its wings had chipped off.

Just then, Derek moved toward her right.

Paula caught herself staring at the pegboard that had been behind him. The calendar hanging there was different. But that wasn't what disturbed her. What caught her attention was the date on top of the page.

December 1997.

The moment the date registered, a cold, heavy blackness moved in, and she no longer felt the floor beneath her feet.

Chapter 15

Paula awoke on the living room couch. Julie Manning knelt on the floor beside her, applying a cold compress to her forehead.

It took her a few moments to get her bearings. The tree, with its blinking lights and glittering ornaments, stood in front of the window to her left. Beneath it, six delicately wrapped gifts sat in a neat line on the red-and-white skirting just below the lights. The TV set was larger than the model she'd remembered the previous night. Brian, slightly heavier and with a considerable sprinkling of gray in his hair, stood in his plaid shirt and workpants, watching her nervously. Derek and Bill stood just a few feet away from the tree, also concerned.

It was definitely the same family and the same house. Her thoughts were cloudy, but she struggled desperately to figure out what had just happened. *I'm* not *going insane. This is the same place they brought me yesterday morning, when my car slipped into the ditch not far from the top of the hill. The same group of nice, caring people I'd just spent Christmas Eve with only a few hours ago. The same place. The same family.*

And Derek. Especially Derek.

But somehow, ten years had slipped by.

By some terrible act of fate, ten years had passed in just a few hours.

Vaguely she remembered the haunting text of the calendar she'd glimpsed just seconds before she'd collapsed.

97

1997. Another decade had gone by in a single night.

Everything had suddenly become so terrifying...

She began wondering once again about this bright new world. A world which, until this moment, had seemed so wonderful—and brighter—and purer—and infinitely more exciting—than the one she'd escaped. This world was much, much better than the cold, dark one that had tried so hard to destroy her. The vile one that had taken Derek away from her. The desolate, bitter inferno covered with darkness and fueled by hatred. And violence. And death. And smothered in desperate, chilling loneliness.

"Feeling better, honey?" Julie asked, watching her intently.

Snapping fully awake, Paula felt the warmth coming back the moment she glimpsed the dear woman's sparkling smile. "I think so... But what happened? Why am I lying here like this?"

"You fainted," Derek said softly. "You were in the hall. You looked at me and fainted."

"Think that might tell ya something?" Bill snickered.

Derek shot him a look.

"I keep tellin' ya, that new cologne won't work too well with girls."

"Shuddup." Derek turned back to her and bent closer. He looked worried. "You okay now?"

"I don't remember what we were doing... What happened last night?"

He blinked, looked more concerned. "You really don't remember?"

A large part of her didn't want to say it aloud. But she knew she had to. She had to find out. One way or the other. "I thought…I thought I spent Christmas Eve here…with you…"

"You did, honey," Julie replied. "Don'tcha remember? Your car went off the road in the snowstorm. Bill and Brian brought you here. You had a nasty bump on your head. I put some mercurochrome on it and bandaged it up."

"I remember…" She'd wanted to ask them why it had been ten years since that all happened but didn't want them to think she was talking nonsense. They might think her injury might be more serious than they'd originally guessed. Although she had no idea what had happened or why, she was fairly certain they wouldn't know anything about ten years slipping by in a single night. They'd obviously aged ten years, but she was reasonably sure that such a long, slow process hadn't taken place in just a few hours.

I'm the one this is happening to, she realized. *Not them.*

She thought it best to keep all this inside. She was hopeful that she'd be able to figure out something later on, when she was feeling better and had regained most of her senses.

"I think we may have kept you up too long, young lady." Looking a little sheepish, Brian came closer. "After the movie, the roasted chestnuts, and the hot cocoa, by the time we all turned in, it was well past one in the morning. We figured that with the bump on your head…" He shrugged.

Yes. That was it. It had to be. The bump on her head. The stress of being forced off the road.

And, of course, that other minor detail of escaping her former world and finding herself in this one…

But just what *was* this other world?

Just when she thought she'd stumbled upon the perfect place, it did the unspeakable and betrayed her. The game plan had mysteriously changed, and without warning. In a single night, it had skipped not days, but years. It had turned itself completely upside-down, upsetting the balance that had beguiled her, making things even more complicated and unimaginable. No longer safe or sated, she found herself totally disoriented, reaching out for some sort of explanation, some semblance of logic that might shed some light on this unsettling phenomenon.

Was the bump on her head the reason that her world had split in two, creating two separate, parallel existences?

Or was this something else entirely?

Was this something that defied all explanation or logic?

What terrified her most of all was that there might not be any answers, any explanations.

Would she be forced to live the rest of her existence in this other world, where nothing made sense? Where time progressed at its own individual, erratic pace?

What would become of her if this happened again?

"Is the compress helping at all, honey?" Julie was talking to her.

"Yes, ma'am. I'm feeling much better."

"Good."

"Well," Brian said, "I called Jack at the garage. He said he can have a truck here sometime a little later, after he and his family have finished opening their presents and had breakfast. That okay with you, Paulie?"

My God. No. It wasn't. It meant leaving. It meant...

She had no idea what it meant. All she could see was the image of herself walking away from these sweet people, leaving their house and getting in her car. Everything else was dark and cold. And terrifying. And—

"Paulie?" It was Brian again.

"Yes. Of course. I'm sorry to be such a bother..."

"No bother at all," he said. Then he left the room and headed for the kitchen.

"Ya hungry?" Derek asked. "We were about to have breakfast."

"Thanks, Rick," she said. "I could use some coffee and—"

"*Rick*?" Bill shot his brother a glance. "No one's called ya *that* since you were a stupid little kid."

Derek didn't say anything for a while. He stared at her, obviously confused. "How'd you know to call me that?"

Her thoughts looped. *Ten years later, Paula. Think. And rationalize.*

Of course he would have outgrown such a childhood quirk once he'd gotten older and realized how much more special the name Derek was...

"No one's called ya that since you were a stupid little kid..."

That was ten years ago...

I know, because I was there...

"I honestly don't know," she said. "I guess...I guess I'm still a little groggy, and my speech isn't quite right. Sorry about that."

It seemed to suffice. He just smiled and nodded. Then he reached out with both arms. "Need some help getting up?"

"I think I'll be okay, thanks." The moment she struggled to sit up, she suddenly felt weaker than she'd realized. Derek quickly knelt before her and helped her. The moment his hands touched hers, she closed her eyes and enjoyed the delicious feel of him. His closeness, his warmth. The exquisite joy of being with him again. Touching him, letting him touch her...

Ten years later. He was almost full grown now. A young man. A considerate, polite, soft-spoken, gorgeous young man.

Then the wrongness of all this rushed right in, interfering with her happy thoughts.

This might not be happening at all. And if it was, it might only be happening in this other world.

But whatever *was* happening felt good. It felt really and truly wonderful. Derek was with her again. Caring for her. Touching her. Helping her.

102

Very shortly, he'd be wrapping his arms around her...

I can't let this end. Somehow, some way, I have to stay here...and live here...and keep that other place from entering this blissful paradise...

She let him pull her into a standing position. She experienced some dizziness at first. Derek held her snugly around the waist, and before she realized it, the dizziness had vanished. He smiled at her, then turned away as the compress slid off her face, landing on the couch cushion. Julie bent and picked it up while Paula let Derek lead her away from the couch.

Moments later, after her equilibrium slowly corrected itself, she realized she could walk on her own. She decided to ignore that obvious but irritating detail and made sure he kept a firm grip on her so he could help her into the kitchen.

Chapter 16

Christmas breakfast filled the bright, warm room with its heavenly aromas.

Large dishes heaped with scrambled eggs, bacon, sausage patties, buttered toast, potato pancakes, blueberry muffins, orange juice and freshly brewed coffee completely covered the center of the long kitchen table.

Before everyone began eating, they stood behind their chairs, looking down. Standing at the head of the table, Brian lowered his head and closed his eyes. Paula also closed her eyes and lowered her head.

Brian cleared his throat. "On this very joyous and wonderful day, let us truly be thankful for the generous bounty we are about to receive. Once again, we're all together on this wonderful occasion. We're healthy and happy, and eager to share our Christmas feast with our very special guest and dear friend, Paula. Amen."

Everyone repeated the amen. Then, as the family pulled out their chairs to sit, Derek, who was sitting beside her, pulled hers out and stood behind it to nudge it forward once she'd taken her seat. It didn't surprise her one bit that he was a gentleman even at that young, awkward age.

Blushing, she smiled and sat. Then he took his own seat beside her.

Suddenly curious about her wound, she reached up and touched the back of her head. There was a slight twinge, but the injury didn't seem nearly as severe. The bandage itself felt smaller. She wondered why the injury was healing so quickly. However, her train of thought was disrupted the moment she heard the clinking of plates and silverware resonating around the table.

"Help yourself, Paula." Brian dumped a large scoop of scrambled egg onto his plate. "With this brood, if ya don't take the initiative—"

"Bill will empty the table in a matter of minutes," Derek finished for his father, then winked at Paula.

"You're one to talk, young man," Julie scolded playfully.

"Yeah." Bill devoured a strip of crispy bacon in one voracious swallow. He jerked a thumb at his younger brother. "That's kind of a perceptible pot you're startin' to grow down there, Brother."

"Perceptible?" Squinting, Brian stared at his older son. "Seriously?" He grunted and shook his head. "You been stickin' your nose in that dictionary while we weren't lookin', boy?"

"Only when I have to," Bill said with a wink.

Frowning, Derek swatted himself sharply in the stomach. It made a loud thumping noise. "Solid as a brick," he said.

"Pretty soon, a concrete block," Bill corrected, and everyone laughed.

While Derek grabbed a blueberry muffin from the steaming basket Julie held out, Paula helped herself to a small serving of scrambled eggs, two pieces of crispy bacon, a sausage patty, and a piece of toast, which she topped with a blot of strawberry marmalade.

"Is that all you're having, honey?" Julie asked.

"For now, thanks." Paula poured a little sugar into her coffee and stirred.

Julie nodded. "I understand, dear. When I was your age, I watched everything I ate, too."

"Lotsa competition out there," Brian said, nibbling on a sausage patty. "A girl's gotta look her best all the time."

"She looks fine to me," Derek said softly as he munched on a piece of toast.

"*Thank* you." Paula felt herself blushing. Out of the corner of her eye, she caught Julie smiling at Derek.

"By the way," Brian said, "how old's that Honda? I couldn't make out the model. The snow had it covered last night."

"It's a two—" She caught herself. She'd almost said 2015. This was only 1997. She knew she had to be careful. Saying the year aloud would have put a damper on the morning festivities.

"Pardon?" Brian asked.

"I think it's around two…two or three years old." She felt her pulse hasten. Then she began worrying about what everyone would think when Jack's son brought his tow truck down the hill and hooked it up to her car. The sun coming brightly into the kitchen window had surely melted some of the snow, exposing more and more of the vehicle. She couldn't remember if the year was displayed anywhere on the body, but the look of the car itself would probably give them pause. And the numbers on the plate would most certainly give evidence of the year.

106

What can I possibly tell them when they realize my car hasn't been manufactured yet? she asked herself, struggling to keep the panic away. *What will they think of me? Will they think I'm some alien visiting earth from the future? Will they be afraid of me? Pull away? Ask me to leave their home? Tell me never to come back?*

Brian nodded. "Figured it was a newer model. Didn't see it too well last night, but I could tell. They've been makin' these foreign jobs pretty sporty nowadays, haven't they?"

"I like mine," she said. "It's very dependable and handles really well."

"Pricey," Derek said.

"They are kind of expensive," she agreed. "But their warrantees are good, and they've got several great mechanics in Pittsburgh."

"What's that model go for?" Bill asked.

Paula's mind reeled.

"That's kinda personal." Brian sent his son a quick glare. "Ya just don't ask a lady how much she paid for somethin'."

"Uh, sorry." Bill looked down at his plate.

"It's all right." Paula sighed in relief. She wanted to kiss the man for bailing her out.

"Where d'ya live in town?" Derek asked.

"Oakland."

Derek grinned. "That's where I'm goin' to college next fall."

"Really?" Like most everything else about Derek, Paula knew where he'd gotten his degree in Finances. But for the sake of propriety, she felt she

107

should express sufficient surprise. "The University of Pittsburgh?"

"Yep." He fitted a small slice of syrup-soaked pancake into his mouth. He suddenly looked thoughtful. "Maybe we'll get to see one another once in a while. How far from the Cathedral of Learning do ya live?"

"Not very. I can probably walk it in fifteen minutes." She felt herself sinking into soft mush again. Now she and Derek were talking about getting together, but it was twenty years in the past. She was thirty-two. He was going to be eighteen. This conversation had become totally unreal…

"Forbes Field used to be out there," he said. "Probably not far from where you live."

"Forbes Field?" Then she remembered. "Oh, yes. The old major league baseball stadium."

"A buddy of mine managed to get hold of one of their seats," Bill said proudly. "Got it for a good price at auction."

"That's right." She remembered something Dad had told her when she was little. "They auctioned off parts of the stadium before they tore it down."

"You remember that?" Brian looked surprised. "This happened *way* before you were born."

"My father told me," she said. "He was always a rabid Pirate fan. He went to Forbes Field a bunch of times when he was little. He said he always took his glove along with him."

"Did he ever get lucky?" Derek asked, wide-eyed.

She smiled at some distant memory. "He told me he almost caught one during practice before a

108

game. But it was from a player from the visiting team."

"My buddy was offered a bunch of money for his seat," Bill said. "Won't sell it, though. It was taken from the right field stands. A front row seat."

"That's where Roberto played," Derek said softly.

"Roberto?" She struggled to remember who they were talking about.

"Roberto Clemente." Derek almost sounded hurt when he'd said the name. "You never heard of Roberto?"

"Well…"

"She's a *girl*," Bill said. "Girls aren't into baseball like us guys."

"I remember hearing his name." She hoped she could get back into their good graces. "Dad mentioned him several times, too. Didn't he have a tremendous throwing arm?"

"Best anyone ever saw," Brian said reverently.

"He had a rifle for a throwin' arm," Bill said.

"No." Derek shook his head. His eyes were as large as silver dollars. "What he had sticking out of his shoulder was a *howitzer*!"

Brian and Bill laughed. Brian said, "You're right, son. I was fortunate enough to have seen him play. That man could peg a runner out at home plate from the right field wall every damn time. He could throw three-hundred-foot line drives all day long."

"And not bat an eye," Derek added with a grin.

"It was a damned shame he died so young," Brian said. "He still had two, maybe three good

109

seasons ahead of him when that plane went down in the Atlantic."

"Enough sports talk," Julie said. "This is Christmas morning. We should be talking about joyous things. Tell us about your family, honey. I'm sure they're missing you this morning. You might wanna call them after breakfast. I don't think the lines are down now. Are they, Brian?"

"Lemme check…" He got up and went over to the wall phone near the kitchen doorway. "I was able to talk to Jack earlier, but ya never know what's gonna happen once all that ice melts." He picked up the receiver and held it close to his ear. Then, after a couple of seconds, he shrugged and replaced it. "They're still up." He came back to the table and sat. He winked at Paula. "You'll be able to call anyone ya please, girl."

"That would be wonderful," she said uneasily. As she sipped her coffee, she wondered how she could possibly squirm her way out of this. She didn't want to call anyone. She was afraid it would jinx everything, ruin her visit here. She was becoming very attached to this new situation and didn't want to do anything that might change things.

Besides, it was a different time. This was 1997—which, according to the other world, was twenty years in the past. Was this world connected to the other? If so, would she be able to communicate with her parents? What would happen when she called them? Would the time discrepancy interfere with the contact?

Twenty years ago, her parents were just five or six years older than she was right now. How would

110

they react when they heard her voice? And it was Christmas morning. Boyd and Tricia would be visiting. Twenty years ago, Tricia was fourteen, Boyd sixteen. What would they do if one of them answered the phone? What would they do when they heard the voice of a woman in her early thirties who said she was their younger sister?

She didn't even think their phone number was the same twenty years ago as it was now. Even if she did remember what it was, what would happen when she tried it? Would it even be working?

Or would she end up talking to some stranger in another county, or state?

She thought about the cellphone she kept in her coat pocket. She knew it would be a colossal mistake to take it out and use it with the Mannings watching. Cellphones had already been invented, but not very many people had them. They were also much larger and bulkier than the slim, tiny model she carried. She hadn't seen evidence of a cell anywhere in this house. She was pretty confident that the Mannings didn't know anything about them.

How could she possibly squirm her way out of this when the time came?

"*Please* tell us about your folks, honey," Julie urged. "Do they live in Oakland, too?"

"Yes. They've been living in the same apartment for the last—well, for a long time."

"Do you have any brothers? Sisters?"

"One of each. They're both older than me."

"Then you're the youngest," Julie said, obviously pleased.

111

"There are only a couple of years between each of us."

"That's how *we* wanted it," Brian said. "However, the wife had other ideas."

"Not really," Julie said, sighing. "I miscarried between the two boys."

"I'm sorry," Paula said.

"No need to be, honey," Julie replied. "I wouldn't change a thing, even if I could. These two are quite a handful, but I wouldn't trade them in for all the tea in China."

"No one else would take 'em," Brian said, laughing.

"Thanks a lump," Bill said.

Paula said nothing. Once again, she found that she couldn't take her eyes off Derek. Right now, he was finishing his last piece of bacon and washing it down with coffee.

Chapter 17

In the living room, the blinking lights from the tree sparkled brightly against the radiant sunshine pushing against the frosted glass of the front window.

The TV was playing the 1951 version of "*A Christmas Carol*," with the volume on low. Brian had taken a VHS tape from the small pile sitting on a shelf of the bookcase and slipped it into the player on top of the TV.

Paula and Julie relaxed on the couch. Bill knelt before the tree, grabbed something from the group of gifts gathered on the skirting, turned, and handed his mother a small, wrapped present. Julie's eyes glistened as she carefully untied the red bow and removed the silver wrappings. She opened the box, removed a broach ring and held it in her hand. For long moments, she couldn't speak. Then, after a deep breath and a slight shudder, she said in a soft, broken voice, "It's *lovely*, boys." She remained sitting there, her eyes shimmering. She even trembled a little. "I just don't...I don't know...what to say..."

"You've wanted one for a long time, babe." Brian watched solemnly as she held it gingerly and gazed hypnotically at it, as if she couldn't believe her own eyes.

"It's so...so *beautiful*..." She remained gawking at it, shaking her head in wonder.

"It's just like the one Grandma had," Derek said.

Nodding, Julie gently slid the broach on the second finger of her right hand. "It…even fits!" Her eyes filled with tears. "I don't know what I'm gonna do with you two," she said softly.

"It's just like the one your mom had," Brian said. "The one that was destroyed in the fire. I know it's not the original, but at least now you've got one…"

"I love it just as much." Sighing, she modeled her hand in front of her, shifting positions and finally resting it in her lap and staring at it. Then she shook her head. "No. I think…I think I love it even more!"

Paula remembered Derek telling her about a fire that had started in his grandmother's basement in Latrobe and set the entire house ablaze within minutes. This happened when Derek was just a boy. His grandmother had been out shopping at the time. By the time she came home, the entire house had burned down to the ground. The poor woman was never the same after that. The total obliteration of her childhood home had destroyed her will to live. And since the fire had taken place less than a year after her husband of thirty-two years had died suddenly of a heart attack, she'd sleepwalked through the next few months, living with Derek's parents, then died peacefully in her sleep at the relatively young age of fifty-eight.

So many sad memories. Paula could almost see the images in Julie's eyes as the other woman sat in silence, gazing at the ring her sons had just given her for Christmas.

Brian's gift was a reciprocating saw, which the boys had given him, bought with money they'd saved from part-time jobs.

"I didn't realize you two could afford one of these," he said, taking his eyes off his new present just long enough to gawk at his smiling sons.

"We couldn't," Derek said with a grin. "That's why we shoplifted it."

"Not funny," Julie said sternly. "Not funny at all."

"He's just kidding," Bill said.

"He'd better be," Brian said.

"Mom helped a little," Derek said.

Brian shot her a look. "Babe? Is this true?"

She shrugged. "Just a few dollars. They had almost the entire amount. The tax thing made it go slightly over."

He shook his head and went back to inspecting his brand-new prize. Picking it up, looking under it, running his hands over its surface, gripping it, checking out its weight, then placing it in his lap and reading the instructions from the attached pamphlet.

"Just make sure you don't use that thing to tear parts of this house apart that don't need messed with," Julie warned. "I don't want to go downstairs one day to do the wash and fall to my death because you suddenly developed one of your notorious wild hairs and decided to get rid of the banister without telling anyone!"

Everyone laughed.

Derek handed Paula a rather large brown envelope.

She gawked at it. "What's this?"

He grinned. "Open it."

Speechless, she did as he suggested. Inside was a large black and white glossy photo of a little league baseball team sitting out in the middle of a baseball diamond. There were two rows of kids, all dressed in their clean uniforms. She could tell which one was Derek almost immediately. He was sitting in the front row, the third boy from the right. His smile was the brightest on the team. Beneath the picture, the words *"The very best Christmas of all!"* was written in ink and signed by Derek.

"When did...when did you have time...for *this*?"

Julie grinned. "That's really an honor, honey. He only had two other prints. I thought he was saving them for when he grew old and would have to live in a rest home. It was definitely his idea."

Grew old...live in a rest home...

The phrase echoed loudly in her head. She could feel herself beginning to crumble.

Just then, Bill, thank God, distracted her before she could embarrass herself. "That was when you were twelve, right?" he asked Derek. "And hit that homerun at the all-star game that won the game?"

Derek was beaming. "Ninth inning. I was down to a—"

"A three-two count," Bill finished. "Yeah. You told us—one or two hundred thousand times before."

Derek shot him a glare. "It was a tense game."

"We know," Brian said. "We were there."

"All three of us," Julie added with a smile.

"Thank you *so* much..." Paula felt her words growing warm and heavy as a lump gathered in her throat.

"Wasn't much." Derek shrugged. "Didn't want ya to feel left out."

"I don't," she said. "I really and truly don't."

"You're not just saying that, are ya, honey?" Julie asked. "We're really enjoying having you here to share Christmas with us."

"I like being here," she said. "In fact, I *love* being here with you. You're all very sweet, wonderful people. And no, I'm not just saying that."

"Good." Brian took a few precious seconds away from inspecting his new reciprocating saw and grinned at her. "I guess it wouldn't be much of a surprise if we told ya we consider you part of our family, would it?"

Paula didn't know what to say. The tears gathering in her eyes made her want to vanish before she could melt into a warm puddle.

"You okay?" Derek asked.

"I'm fine." Sniffing, she turned away from him and wiped away the tears.

The phone in the kitchen rang.

"That's prob'ly Jack." Brian laid down his new saw gently on top of its box. Then got up, left the room and disappeared in the kitchen.

Paula's pulse raced as she heard him talking softly on the phone.

He's talking about me. My car. This beautiful visit is coming to an end. This wonderful, joyous accident is soon going to be over...

About ten seconds later, Brian hung up and came back out into the hall. "That was Jack. He's on his way down with the tow truck."

Sniffing back the rest of her tears, Paula got up from the couch. She really didn't want to go through with this but saw no other way out of it. *I belong here*, she reminded herself. *I really and truly belong here. I don't want Jack to tow my car. I don't want to leave this family and drive away. Once I leave, I'm afraid I'll never be able to come back. I want to stay here forever, and I want to live with this beautiful family and fall in love with Derek all over again, and—*

"Is something wrong, dear?" Julie asked.

"You look…sad," Derek said softly.

Shaking herself out of her fantasy, she forced a smile. "I'm fine." Then, clutching the precious photo against her bosom, she said, "I guess I'll go get my things. I'll be ready to leave when he's finished checking out my car."

Checking out my car…

The grim reality of the situation slammed into her.

What would the man do when he realized he was looking at a vehicle that wouldn't be produced for another decade? What would he say? What would he think? Would he tell Brian? What would Brian say when he found out?

Would this jinx everything? Would it change her destiny? Would it bring back the old world?

What on earth would happen?

"Paula?" Julie looked worried.

118

Snapping out of her inner torment, she forced herself to return to the here and now. She didn't want to. But she knew she had no choice.

"I'm okay." She sent over a smile that took every bit of strength she could find within herself.

No one said anything as she left the room and shuffled down the hall.

Chapter 18

Before closing her overnight case, Paula picked up Derek's group photo once again.

He was sitting on the bench with the rest of the boys. But even though there were more than thirty boys in the photo, there was something about him that made him much more special than the rest of his teammates. She couldn't tell if it was his eyes, his smile, or the way he was sitting. All she knew was that the moment her eyes saw the photo, Derek's image reached out for her and pulled her in.

She was obviously overwhelmed and knew she would remain so. A family who'd never seen her before had taken her into their home and shared their Christmas with her. They'd treated her as one of them. It was as if they'd known her all their lives.

How incredibly wonderful…and yet very strange…

Yes. Stranger than she could ever have imagined.

They brought me into their home. They dressed and tended to my wound. They fed me, talked to me, laughed with me, shared their holiday with me. They'd considered me a member of their family.

But I was a member of their family. Derek and I were in love and were about to be married. Of course they'd consider me a member of their family.

But not in this world.

In this very strange world, they hadn't met her yet. In this fascinating, mysterious world, half a lifetime of events had not yet happened. Derek was still a young man. A sweet, honest, respectful, honorable young man. And he still had half a lifetime to live before...

Enough of this. If she stayed in this room much longer, she'd go mad. Her mind was working in overload, and if she kept this up, she wouldn't be able to see an end or reach any sort of conclusion. Besides, the Mannings would worry and eventually look in on her to see if everything was all right. She didn't want them worrying. She decided to get ready to leave this room—as well as this beautiful, caring family—before she did or said something stupid.

But once again, she wondered where she would go once she got back into the Honda. Would she have to leave this world to return to the other? The dark, unpleasant one she never wanted to see again?

How could she possibly avoid that other world?

More importantly, how could she stay here? As friendly and as accommodating as the Mannings were, she just wasn't one of them. She wasn't a relative. They didn't even know her. Since it was twenty years ago, they hadn't even met her. What could she possibly do once she left this house? What would happen if she got in the Honda, drove back up the hill, turned around at the sharp bend and came right back down?

It seemed simple, didn't it? And very logical. After all, she'd just rounded the bend on her way here when everything in her world turned upside-down. Why couldn't she just stop short of it on this side so she could stay here forever?

Would it work? Or was she hallucinating?

She reached up and felt the back of her head. The lump was still there, but much smaller than even minutes ago, when she'd examined it at the breakfast table. It no longer felt tender, and the throbbing had stopped.

She wondered once again how it had healed so quickly.

Just then, it dawned on her that if the wound had almost healed, there should be no reason for any more hallucinations, or wild notions.

After all, she'd been thinking very clearly. She knew her name, where she was from, and why she'd come here. She didn't know exactly what had happened, or how she'd entered this strange existence, but she knew what had happened to cause it. And since she was aware of all that, it only stood to reason that she should be able to decide what to do from this point on.

It was settled. When she walked out of this room, she was going to tell these wonderful people that she never wanted to leave them. She wanted to live here with them forever. She would do whatever they asked, whenever they asked. She would be no trouble. And she would promise them that they would never regret their decision to let her stay with them.

What would they do? Would they accept her? Think she was crazy?

Or would they tell her to leave anyway?

They weren't the type of people to do something like that. They were sweet and kind and considerate. They liked her. They'd even told her they considered her part of their family. They'd tell her it was all right, that she could stay with them as long as she wished.

They had to. They couldn't change their minds and turn their backs on her. It just wasn't how they were.

Her mind made up, she gently closed and latched her case. Then she went over to the window and looked out.

The storm had passed. The late afternoon sun had melted more snow. The short row of slender, dying icicles hanging from the top of the windowpane dripped steadily.

She turned away from the window and scanned the room. She'd already made her bed but decided it wasn't neat enough. She immediately pulled the bed sheets tighter at the corners and propped up the pillows better. This done, she backed up and inspected her work.

Not bad. At least Julie wouldn't have to redo it.

Somewhat satisfied, she turned back to the window.

It only took her a moment to realize something was very different.

The sun still shone, but there was no longer any sign of melting icicles. The window itself wasn't fogged up or smeared, as it had been just seconds ago.

What was going on?

Why had the window's appearance changed so drastically in the time it took her to tend to her bed and—

No. The frightening realization stabbed her sharply in the chest.

Things had changed again. In an instant. Just like the last time.

The window. The world outside. The storm.

This meant—

No. It couldn't be. Not again!

She gawked at the door and backed up. No. She wouldn't go out there again. She couldn't. She'd stay right here in this comfortable little room, where everything was just as it had been moments before and would stay that way. Outside might have changed, but everything in here remained the same, and she wanted it to stay this way forever. From here, she could visualize everything else being the same, too. Derek and Bill and Brian and Julie would still be in the living room, enjoying Christmas morning. Brian's friend Jack or one of Jack's sons would be tending to the Honda. Julie would be staring at her brand-new broach ring, Brian his brand-new reciprocating saw. All Paula had to do was stay here and wait and see if things would return to the way they were and always would be—

A soft knock on the door.

"Honey?" Julie's voice. "You all right?"

She cleared her throat, but her voice came out pitifully anyway. "I'm…I'm fine…"

"Jack's out there with your car. He'd like to see you so he can talk to you about it."

"Be right out."

"Take your time."

Silence.

She stood there, trembling as she gawked at the door, expecting it to…to—

124

To what? Open itself? Change into something else? Explode in a million pieces?

You've got to do this, her inner voice told her. *It was inevitable that the moment you stumbled into this strange, wonderful world, you were destined to see more and more of it the longer you stayed. Now that you've remained here and have seen ten years—then twenty—go by in an instant, you know that this world is not real, It never really was. It's an imaginary world with imaginary people, and the longer you stay here, the more imaginary you yourself will become.*

She reached out for the door and stopped. Then stared at her hand and willed it to disappear. To become hazy. She closed her eyes and concentrated. *Imaginary. Not real. Turn younger. Twenty years younger should do it for now. Then Derek and I will be the same age again. Turn. Do it. Now...*

She opened her eyes. Her heart sank, and she sighed in defeat. Her hand remained the same. Like the rest of her, it stayed real.

I want to be imaginary, she told herself. *I don't want to be real anymore.*

Do you? Do you really?

I think I do...

It won't work for you, came the reply. *You're not imaginary. Living in this world will not work for you. You've got a life of your own. A career. A family of your own...*

Maybe I don't care about the other stuff. Maybe I truly want to live in this world. Maybe I feel more like myself. Maybe I'll feel even better the longer I stay here. Maybe I feel the love I lost, that wonderful love that was ripped viciously out of my heart the moment Derek was taken from me. Maybe I want that love to stay with me the rest of my life. Maybe I'll never feel whole again unless this love remains with me...

Do you honestly think this world will be here much longer? the voice inside her persisted.

Yes, she replied, holding back a sudden flare of rage. *Yes. It will be. It will always be here. It has to be. I won't let it vanish. I won't let it go anywhere!*

And what happens to you when you turn your back one instant and discover that it's no longer there? That you're *no longer there?*

Yes. Unfortunately, her inner voice made sense. Despite the growing love she felt for this world, for this family, she knew full well that it couldn't be real. None of it was real. The house. The family. Derek. Julie. None of this could possibly be real. It was much too wonderful to be real.

This was the past. And everyone knew that it was impossible to live in the past.

"I have to go back..." Her voice had become a strained whisper. The final words of someone sensing imminent death. She felt the tears gathering the moment the dreaded words had left her mouth. "As much as I don't want to, as much as I want to become part of this special place, I know I have to leave. I have to return to that cold, dark world that wants to destroy me."

She found Kleenex in her bag, wiped her eyes and blew her nose. Her heart was pumping madly as she approached the door. It was only ten feet from the bed, but it took her forever to get to it. She kept stopping, hoping she was wrong. That this new existence was indeed real.

"*You'll never know for sure until you leave this room*," her inner voice told her.

She tried convincing herself that she was doing the right thing after all. That it was the only thing she could possibly do. And that if she didn't do it, she'd be doomed to stay in this room and wait for whatever frightening changes came about in this strange world.

Taking a deep breath, she squared her shoulders and approached the door. With trembling fingers, she reached out and grasped the doorknob. Then, flinching at its coldness, she carefully opened the door. Her legs were heavy and stiff as she shuffled down the hall.

Just moments later, they turned into warm mush when she caught the shocking image at the end of the hall.

Chapter 19

Derek was standing behind the living room couch, staring at the tree.

The couch was different. So were the tree and the ornaments.

And so was Derek.

He was slightly taller than when she'd last seen him. Right now, he seemed to be the height he was when she'd first met him in the other world, at just under six feet.

Paula stopped a foot short of the kitchen doorway. This time, when she stared at the space where the calendar usually hung, she saw that it wasn't there. She didn't know if that was a good thing, but for some reason, it made her sigh in relief. She turned back to Derek.

From the back, his hair looked the same but was slightly longer. He seemed just a few pounds thinner than she remembered from the other world. Otherwise, he was definitely the same wonderful man she'd fallen in love with and had lost much too soon.

Finding her voice, she managed a soft, shaky, "H-Hello…"

He turned and grinned, and she found herself melting just as she had in the other world, whenever their eyes met. He was the same Derek she'd known and loved, but just a handful of years younger. Mid- or late twenties, she decided, noticing the facial hair beginning to grow on his upper lip and chin. She'd never seen him with a mustache but knew he'd look good in one. He always looked good. And as she continued staring, she found that she could think of nothing else to say. The only thing she could do was stand there and tremble. This was entirely too strange. Yet, it was so incredibly wonderful.

Derek, my darling, she wanted so much to say, *you've come back to me...*

Although she'd stopped trembling, her legs had gone numb. So had her arms. Forcing herself to stay in control, she struggled to stand straight and proud. Collapsing or fainting right now would not be very cool. She began to sense an inner peace—as well as a comforting inner warmth—consuming her. The tears threatened to flow. She forced them back, promising herself that she'd find the time to cry sometime later on, once this blessed, beautiful moment had ended.

"Are you ready to leave?" he asked in a soft voice that sounded just like the man she'd fallen in love with such a very short time ago.

Fearful that her voice would fail her, she nodded.

"Let me take your bag." Without waiting for a reply or protest, he came right over. Then, bending slightly, he reached for her overnight bag.

As he bent, his head had moved closer, and she took in the familiar sweet scent of his shampoo. She closed her eyes and bathed herself in this delicious splendor, remembering things, events. Treasured memories that, like their love, would always remain, and would never die. And as these memories drifted past, she realized that even though she'd lost this wonderful man in that other world, the images would forever stay with her. They'd become part of her. Her essence, her being. Nothing would ever take them away.

"You okay?"

Startled, she opened her eyes.

He'd straightened and was standing close, his face less than two feet away. She wanted so much to kiss him. To wrap her arms around him. To bury her hands in his hair and pull him closer to her... But she didn't want to spoil or change this tender moment. She was frightened that it would end much sooner than she wished anyway, so why hasten the inevitable? This strange world, which she'd fallen in love with and held onto so stubbornly, had betrayed her. She found that she could no longer trust it. The end was coming—this was painfully evident—and she wanted to savor each delicious moment she had left.

"Something wrong?" he asked.

She couldn't stop smiling at him. "No. Everything's just perfect." She was surprised her voice had decided to start working again.

"Mom and Dad went to the store to pick up a few things. They'll be back in just a few minutes. They'd like to see you before you leave."

"They went to the store on Christmas Day?"

He blinked. "You've got your days mixed up. This is Christmas Eve."

"Really?"

He nodded.

She found that she couldn't speak. Once again, she'd been tricked and knew that she could no longer believe anything she saw or heard. As much

130

as she hated the other world and wanted to stay away from it forever, she realized that she was once again surrounded by guile and deceit.

"Are you sure you're okay?" Derek seemed genuinely concerned.

Still smiling, she nodded. "I'm fine now."

"Good." He seemed pleased.

"Where's Bill?" She suddenly noticed his brother's absence.

"He's on his way. He had to tend to something before he could leave the office. He should be here in about an hour." He grinned. "One thing the Manning boys do, if nothing else? They always spend Christmas with the folks."

"Your parents are very lucky." She thought of her own family and felt a pang of sadness.

"Well, Jack has your car ready to go. Let's get your stuff in it. Mom and Dad should be back by the time you're ready to leave." He moved past her, making his way for the front door. She watched him as he moved in his usual brisk gait, carrying her bag as if it weighed nothing. As he approached the door, he turned. "You're coming, aren'tcha?"

She took in a breath. "Yes." Then she began moving. Luckily, her feet and legs obeyed her.

Derek opened the front door and stepped back, waiting for her to go first.

Just as she took a few steps toward him, she glanced toward the kitchen and saw that the calendar hung in a different place. She stopped cold when her gaze focused on the top of the page.

December 2007.

Once again, her heart climbed up to her throat.

This world had tricked her once again. Ten more years had passed since she'd gone into the spare room to collect her things.

"What's wrong now?"

She smiled at him and fought very hard to keep her composure. "I'm just saying bye...to your house."

"You'll be back, won'tcha?"

"I hope so. One day..."

He kept his smile. "I hope so, too."

Barely holding herself together, she turned to him. Before she could say anything, he'd moved toward her and took her right hand. His touch was strong and warm. She closed her eyes. A lifetime of treasured memories whizzed by in an instant. She felt warmth and contentment, and a sense of happiness she had only experienced with this man in the other world. Her whole body tingled, and with the warmth came one last bright vision of Derek. This time he was smiling at her and telling her one last time that he loved her, would always love her, and would be waiting for her when her own time came.

Just then, the warmth of his touch vanished.

"I'm really sorry about that..."

His voice snapped her out of it. She opened her eyes.

He remained standing close, looking down. He'd lowered his arm. "I didn't mean to... That is, I really didn't—"

"It's all right."

"I've never done anything like that before. Not to someone I've only known just a short time—"

132

"I understand. Believe me, it was all right."

"Honestly?"

"Yes."

He went silent again. She could tell he was trying to think of a better way of explaining himself. A few moments later, he cleared his throat. "I just had this sudden urge. I needed to touch you. I can't explain it. It was this feeling I had…"

"I'm glad you did."

His eyes grew. "Really?"

"Yes." She sensed herself crumbling again. Her legs had become weak, unstable.

"You're not just…saying that?"

She shook her head.

He stared at her a while longer, possibly to determine if she was telling him the truth. He must have realized she was. Then he smiled. "Can I tell you something?"

"Yes. Please."

"I've had this strange feeling ever since I first saw you. When Bill helped you out of your car. It's like…like I knew you before. A long time ago."

She took a deep breath and fought the sudden approaching dizziness. "Really?"

He nodded. "I can't help feeling that I might have known you in…in another life. I know that must sound crazy, but…" He frowned and looked troubled. "Does that make any sense to you?"

"Yes. It does."

"I don't suppose…I don't suppose you feel the same way. Do you?"

She struggled hard to keep the tears at bay. "Yes. I really do."

"Strange, isn't it?"

She nodded and swallowed the lump that had been gathering in her throat.

He shrugged and, after a few awkward moments, smiled sheepishly. "I get some weird notions sometimes. Always have. Bill thinks I'm mental."

"I don't think you're mental at all. It's probably because I think about the very same things."

He gazed at her a while longer. Then sighed and turned toward the doorway.

Collecting herself, she forced her legs to start working again. She slipped by him and went out onto the front porch.

It was a cold morning. The ground had turned white with a gentle dusting of fresh snow. But it showed no evidence of a winter storm. No icicles were dangling from the windowpanes.

She approached the front steps.

"Paula?"

"Yes?" She turned.

He suddenly seemed different. Older, as he'd been the last day she'd seen him in the other world. His face had also changed, his eyes very bright, his smile dazzling. The dimple on his cheek had become larger, and she could have sworn she saw his eyes sparkle.

The sun, perhaps? Or was it something else?

It made her wonder if any of this was real.

"I have to tell you something else." His voice sounded strange. As if it was coming from another place.

"Yes?"

"I'm okay," he said. "And soon you'll be okay, too."

"Pardon me?" It seemed an odd thing to say, especially at that moment. As she gazed longingly at him, she thought she saw him changing again. The sparkle in his eyes had gone. His smile had diminished a little, and his dimple had gone back to its original size.

"I said the roads are okay," he said, a little louder this time. "The storm wasn't bad at all. You'll be okay, too."

She nodded in spite of her confusion. She'd obviously heard him wrong the first time. That was really no surprise. After what he'd said in the house earlier, she knew to expect strange things as long as she remained here.

"Thank you again." She waved.

"It was no problem at all."

Then, in spite of her desire to go back to him, she knew she had to end this delicious moment. She turned back to the steps.

The Honda sat facing the house just twenty feet away, a thin dusting of white on its roof.

Derek passed her on the way to the car. "Jack Junior brought it down and made sure the battery was good and everything else was in running order. He said nothing was wrong with it. He did wonder what model it was. Said he never saw anything quite like it before. Neither have I. Sure is a fancy model."

"They only made them a short time, then discontinued them." She couldn't think of anything else to say that would make sense.

"Figured as much." Derek opened the passenger door and carefully placed her overnight bag on the seat. Then, straightening, he closed the door, circled the car and opened the driver's side for her.

Her feet turned mushy again as she approached her car. Slipping by him, she fought down the urge to wrap her arms around him. She still suspected none of this was real, but somehow it didn't matter. Some inner sense told her that if she touched him again, it would destroy the fabric of what had already happened. She forced herself into the seat. Then, dropping her handbag on the floor in front of the passenger seat, she fastened her seat belt.

"Have a safe trip." Derek stood outside her door, smiling down at her.

"But your parents... I really hoped they'd be here before I left."

He glanced toward the main road. "I guess they're taking a little longer than they thought." He shrugged. "I'll tell them you gave them your best."

"I'll really...miss you." Her heart tugged the moment she'd said it.

"We'll see one another again," he said, still smiling.

She could tell by the expression in his eyes that he'd meant what he said. "Yes. We will. I just hope it's soon."

He shrugged. "One never knows. Time slips by so quickly..."

Yes. It certainly did. It slipped by even quicker than most people could ever imagine.

136

"I'll never forget all you've done for me." Words seemed inadequate. She realized she was talking to the image of someone who had once been the most wonderful part of her life. An image that would not last much longer. She gazed into Derek's beautiful eyes and felt herself crumbling because she knew this moment would never return. And although she knew she had no control over what was about to happen, she still didn't want it to end, and longed to tell him that she didn't really want to leave. She wanted to stay here with them for as long as she could. Her other world scared her, saddened her… And she wanted to stay here forever.

You have to go, her mind told her.

I don't want to.

This isn't real. You have to go.

"We really enjoyed having you stay with us," Derek said. "It's a shame you couldn't spend Christmas with us, but you've obviously got other business to tend to. And since your car's ready to go…" He shrugged.

"But I'd love to…to—"

Then she stopped.

"Pardon?"

"Nothing." She had to struggle to stay strong. It took every fiber in her being to look at him and not fall into a million pieces. She feared something horrible would happen if she let herself go. That even though her love was pure, this was all wrong. "Once again, thanks for everything, and tell your parents I was sorry I couldn't have seen them before I left. Tell Bill I'm sorry I missed him, too."

He smiled and pushed her door shut. He stood there a few moments, smiling at her, and she wondered if there was something in his smile that had come from a different place. Perhaps it was the place his spirit had gone to when he was taken from her. She had no idea. All she knew was that there was something in his smile that, despite this heart-breaking departure, made her feel warm inside. Something that made her feel almost as if a strange happiness awaited them both sometime later on.

Then, just as quickly as the warmth and feeling of happiness had entered her spirit, it vanished. She suddenly felt sad and lonely as she watched him walk back to the house.

Her gaze stayed on him even as he went up the front steps. Then, feeling the tears coming back, she reached down to start the car and flicked it in reverse. Just as she began backing up, she turned back to the house. To see him one last time. To smile at him, give him one last final wave.

Derek was standing there, waving at her.

And fading...

"Derek?" She slammed the Honda into park and groped for the door handle. As she struggled to get out, she realized she was trapped in the seat. Her seat belt remained fastened. She glanced at him again. He'd faded even more. "Dammit!" She wrestled with the snap until it clicked open, releasing her.

She grabbed the door handle. And glanced at him one last time.

Derek had vanished.

The panic swept up her back. The beginnings of a giant scream built up hotly in her lungs.

For tense moments Paula sat there, trembling and gawking in utter fear and disbelief at the empty porch. Her mind looped and her thoughts cascaded wildly. *Come back, Derek. Please come back. I need to see you one last time. Please come back just for one more second!*

Then, during her growing madness, she rubbed her eyes and hoped his image would return. That he'd be standing on the porch again, waving at her.

An eternity later, she opened her eyes.

Haze...

Then brightness.

Then...a feeling of movement.

As she reached the bottom of the hill, she applied her foot to the brake, pulled off the road and turned into the gravel drive of the Mannings' house.

She eased to a stop facing the house, put the car into park, and flicked off the ignition. Then sat there for what seemed a long time, staring at the front porch, wondering why she suddenly felt so strange.

Her thoughts were cloudy, but she could vaguely remember sliding off the road just moments ago and stopping abruptly in a ditch not too far up the hill.

But why do I feel like I've just woken up?

She'd hit her head. Yes. That would explain it. She'd whacked her head on the head rest, and it had dazed her. She recalled sitting there for a while, her head back, eyes closed, getting her nerves under control.

That might explain her confusion.

139

Had she been unconscious? Would this explain the sensation that she'd just woken up?

Then, during her inner turmoil, she saw the front door of the house opening.

Derek's parents stepped outside and stood on the porch, watching her.

Chapter 20

Derek's mother, looking as frail as Paula had seen her at the funeral, stood beside Bill, who also hadn't changed much at all.

Both were pale and obviously weak and fragile from the stress of grieving. They stood quite close to one another, holding each other by the arm. Paula wanted to cry when she saw how much they were hurting.

However, she sensed that the best thing she should do was get out of the car and greet them. And forget about everything she'd rehearsed on her trip over. And just tell them what was in her heart. But as she opened the door and stepped out onto the gravel, she sensed something else. Something she couldn't immediately explain.

It was almost as if time had abruptly stopped. A cold breeze whispered past, tingling her cheeks and sweeping her hair in front of her face. As she pushed it gently away from her eyes, Paula noticed that the air smelled different. The day appeared brighter, the air slightly more chilled than it had been before, when she'd first left the apartment in Oakland.

When had that been? For some reason, her mind had become cloudy again. It felt almost like she'd been here very recently, although that hardly seemed likely. The last time Derek had brought her here for a visit had been several months ago.

Why did it seem like something else had just happened?

Why do I feel almost like I was leaving?

She'd just gotten here, hadn't she? It was early in the morning, but something about all this felt strange. As if she'd just left the Manning house and walked over to her car?

Why was she so confused? And why did she feel so differently about everything?

For one thing, she sensed that much of her grief had been lifted from her shoulders and carried away. What was the reason? And where did all her grief go?

More importantly, what had made it go away? And why?

Perhaps coming to see Derek's parents had become a sort of medicine. Or maybe her grief had somehow dissolved itself sometime during the trip. It made no sense, but neither did this sudden confusion that had been filling her head since she'd gotten out of the car.

She wondered if it had something to do with her hitting her head when she'd gone off the road.

Or maybe it had been the result of her sensing Derek's spirit in her bedroom earlier that morning.

Stranger things had happened. For one thing, the act of sensing Derek's presence had enabled her to leave the apartment for the first time since his funeral. It had also encouraged her to put on her regular clothes. And get in her car and drive away from the city.

Maybe this had all been necessary. Maybe it had taken Derek's spirit—or hallucination—to pull her out of that thick black blanket of grief that had been smothering her. And during the trip here, the last of it might have been ripped away with the snowstorm, bringing her back to the real world while shedding at least some of the grief.

It didn't matter, did it? What mattered was that she now felt a strong urge to live. It had only been six weeks since Derek had died, but for some reason, she now felt she could break out of the cocoon she'd created for herself when she'd lost him. The man she'd loved with all her heart was gone—she realized that. She also realized that it was going to take her a lot longer than six weeks to fully recover from this. She feared she never might fully recover at all. Derek was her soul mate. No one could recover fully when their soul mate was taken from them.

But for some reason she could not understand, she now felt that he was at peace, and happy. She also felt that her sensing his spirit in her bedroom could actually have been her subconscious struggling to help her regain her life.

She had no idea what really happened. She only knew that something had. Whether it was some sort of miracle that had made this possible, she didn't know. Perhaps the brightness of his aura had returned from wherever his spirit now was to remove her grief from her and replace it with renewed happiness and a wash of fresh hope that would stay with her for the rest of her days.

"*They need to see you,*" her inner voice had told her. "*And you need to see them.*"

That happened just hours ago, didn't it?

The only thing she cared about was that she honestly believed Derek was at peace and had come back to reassure her. The circumstances that had enabled his return would never fully be clear, but the fact that she no longer felt smothered in a heavy blanket of sadness was enough to make her realize that some things happening in this life weren't meant to be fully understood.

Miracles did not have to be understood. If you were one of the few lucky ones to have actually witnessed a miracle, it was only important that you believed it and didn't ask questions. Because, as with all wonderful things, it would eventually fade away and turn into a hazy, warm memory. But even though its presence would fade over the years, it would still bring a sudden smile to your lips later on, just a moment or two after you'd closed your eyes and drifted off into a restful sleep.

She knew now that things were only as dark as you'd let them be. She supposed that if she remained receptive to what life had planned for her, she should ask no questions. The important thing was that she understood that life could be something wonderful and blissfully mysterious.

I've come back, she realized, smiling at the two people who'd been responsible for bringing into the world the man she would love as long as she lived. She knew Derek would not want her to spend the rest of her life grieving for him. She didn't fully understand that before, but she certainly did now.

Julie and Brian slowly descended the front steps and came over. Brian was looking at her car on the passenger side. He grimaced. "Slide off the road up there? Just beyond the bend?"

Paula circled the front of the Honda. She'd been right; she really had run off the road. The snow tires were caked with mud and snow, and there was a noticeable dent on the body just behind the rear tire.

This would certainly explain that smack on the back of her head. It might also explain the strange grogginess she'd experienced a few moments ago. She reached up and touched the back of her head. It was a little tender, but nothing to worry about. There was hardly even a bump to speak of. And, more important, no blood.

"I sure did," she said, and wondered once again if she'd been knocked out temporarily. For a moment she thought she remembered someone walking up the hill to help her. A boy? Or was he a young man?

Probably just my imagination. Or some shadowy images resulting from the bump on my head.

"Good thing you didn't slide off and slip down the hill," he said. "You mighta landed in the creek. Or you coulda slammed into the guard rail and did serious damage to your car. We woulda had to call Jack, have 'im tow the car and take it up to his garage. Then he'd need a week or so to do the body work. That is, unless you wanted to have it towed to your Honda place in town. Either way, woulda been pricey. That tiny dent you picked up could run ya five hundred, easy."

"I guess I was just lucky."

Brian nodded. "Lucky's right. Coulda been hit with that arctic storm on your way here. It's comin'

145

as we speak." He glanced up at the sky. "Figure it oughta be here by this evening."

Arctic storm. Run off the road. Tow.

Something felt very strange was happening. Something she couldn't quite grasp. She thought once again about that figure walking up the hill.

I must have dreamed that or something. The whole thing felt very odd.

"Enough of that chatter," Julie said, sniffing. "Come here, honey." She held out her arms. Paula fell into them.

After several minutes of hugs and tender, heartfelt tears, Julie finally pulled away and applied a Kleenex to her glistening red eyes. Then, in a soft, broken voice, she said, "Please tell us you'll want to stay with us for at least a little while."

"I'd be honored."

"It's all right with your parents?" Julie shrugged. "I mean, it *is* Christmas Eve…"

She remembered Dad's sadness as he sat at the kitchen table that same morning, the bottle of Scotch at his elbow. Staring at her with his tired, blood-shot eyes, knowing that as much as he loved her, he couldn't possibly help her. "They'll understand, believe me."

"Good. That storm ain't gonna wait." Brian glanced up at the sky again.

"You brought your things?" Julie asked.

"I've got my overnight bag."

Brian was staring at the house. Then he sighed and shook his head. Tears glinted in his eyes. "I coulda sworn I just saw him standin' there."

"Again?" Julie asked softly.

146

He nodded. "Seemed different this time."

"Different? How?"

He shrugged. "Dunno. Stronger. Clearer." He took a breath. "Closer. Made me feel…well, not so sad."

Julie went silent as she stared at the porch for a few moments. "This morning I had this strong feeling that he's happy. And at peace. I can't explain it. It's just a feeling, I guess."

"Christmas was special to him," Brian said. "Maybe it's that."

"Wouldn't surprise me," Julie said.

Paula found herself staring at the front porch as well.

"C'mon, honey." Julie sniffed back her tears. "Enough of that. We need to help Paulie."

Brian nodded and wiped his eyes.

"I can get them, thanks. I'll just be a second." She hurried back to the Honda, opened the door, and bent to grab her handbag and overnight bag. As she pulled them toward her, she caught a glimpse of herself in the rearview. She groaned. Her hair was a mess. She'd obviously been knocked around more than she'd thought. A quick run-through with the comb might help. She sat down behind the wheel and opened her bag. And started.

A large envelope lay flat on top of her things.

Funny. She didn't remember packing an envelope. She picked it up and opened it. And gasped.

It was a photo of Derek's Little League team, obviously taken more than twenty years ago. Beneath the picture, the words, *The very best*

Christmas of all!" were written in ink and signed by Derek.

Brian and Julie came over. "Something wrong, honey?" Julie asked.

Without a word, she handed them the photo.

They both gawked at it and froze.

Shaking himself out of it, Brian whispered, "When did he give ya this, Paulie?"

She tried remembering, but for some strange reason, she'd drawn a complete blank. To make things even more confusing, she didn't remember putting it in her bag.

But she had to have done it, didn't she? Who else could have put it there?

"That's just it. I don't remember."

"This was taken when he hit that homer at the all-star game." Brian grinned proudly, wet eyes and all. "He musta been around twelve, judgin' by how he looks here." Brian handed it back. "Ya don't remember when he gave it to ya?"

"I know I should, but I just don't." She stared at it, struggling to remember. Nothing would come. Derek had given her a lot of presents during the two years they were together. She could clearly remember just about all of them.

Why was this any different?

"It had to have been last Christmas," Brian said.

"Why do you say that?" she asked.

He shrugged. "Look how he signed it."

"Yes, but it doesn't tell me—"

"You two were together your first Christmas, right? You came here for Christmas dinner, but the

148

next morning, you both went back to Oakland. Somethin' about an office party at Derek's company that same night, if I recall correctly…"

"I remember that," Julie said.

"But we spent two Christmases together," Paula said. "Maybe it was last Christmas…"

"It had to have been the first Christmas," Brian said. "You two didn't know one another as well, so you weren't as close. Otherwise, Derek woulda signed it more personal."

"Yes." That made perfect sense. But she still couldn't remember Derek giving her the photo.

After a short while, Julie said, "We can talk about this later. Let's go inside and get warm. It's getting cold out here."

"That storm wants to be here for Christmas, too." Brian shivered and shook his head.

Still obsessing about the photo, Paula got out, grabbed her bags and closed the door. As she slung the strap of her handbag over her shoulder, Brian took the overnight case from her. He said, "He was really proud of that picture. And he dreamed about that homer. Told us about it every chance he had. For *days*…"

"We didn't think he'd part with any of them," Julie said. "That's really an honor, honey. He only had two other prints."

Why does this conversation sound so familiar? she wondered. Then, just when she thought she might have remembered something, Julie said, "We'll go inside now and have some breakfast and a fresh pot of nice, hot coffee."

"And blueberry muffins?" Brian asked, both brows raised.

Julie sighed patiently. "Yes, dear. We'll have blueberry muffins."

He licked his lips. "I think I could eat a couple. Maybe even three or four."

Julie gave him a stern look. "Listen here, buster. You'd better save a little of that appetite for Christmas dinner. I'm making my famous pork roast, and you know Bill won't like it one bit when he gets here and finds out you've already stuffed yourself silly on too much food. You know how he loves you to fight him for the crust slivers."

"Fat chance of him ever winnin' *that*," he said, laughing.

Their spirits somewhat lifted, the three of them walked arm-in-arm to the front porch.

As Paula climbed the steps, she was certain she caught a brief image of Derek standing right there in front of the door, smiling at her.

I'll love you forever, my angel, she thought, smiling through a fresh batch of warm tears as she followed his parents inside.

OTHER WORKS BY DAVID BERARDELLI

THE APPRENTICE
THE WAGON DRIVER
DEMON CHASER
DEMON CHASER II
STEPPING OUT OF MY GRAVE
ESCAPE CLAUSE
FATAL INNOCENCE
THE FUNNY DETECTIVE
JUST A SIMPLE ERRAND
COLORS
WORKING FOR A MOB BOSS
AND DARKNESS FELL
AFTER DARKNESS FELL
DEMON CHASER III
IN ANOTHER REALM
BEYOND RECOGNITION
LOOKING FOR A DEAD GUY
THE NIGHTMARE COLLECTOR
HIDDEN
BEYOND GUILT
DEMON CHASER IV
DEMON CHASER V
ENLIGHTENMENT
A RIPPLE IN TIME
HUNTING THE TALL BLONDE

AWAKENED
REDEMPTION
THE PLANNING COMMITTEE
WINTER SCENE

Titles available through:
Fiction4All

www.ingramcontent.com/pod-product-compliance
Lightning Source LLC
Chambersburg PA
CBHW011512170626
46810CB00009B/3335